Bernice Rubens

I SENT A LETTER TO
MY LOVE

First published in Abacus by
Sphere Books Ltd 1980
30–32 Gray's Inn Road, London WC1X 8JL
Reprinted 1982
Copyright © 1975 by Bernice Rubens

First published in Great Britain by
W. H. Allen & Co. Ltd., 1975

Printed and bound in Great Britain by
Cox & Wyman Ltd, Reading

For Beryl

'For thou shalt see the land afar off;
but thou shalt not go thither.'

Deuteronomy **XXXII**:52

Part One

When she was a child, Amy Evans would steal into the sweet shop on the way home from school and buy a stick of rock. It was forbidden, strictly forbidden, murderous to the teeth that the good Lord gave you, her Mam would say, and as it turned out her Mam was right, for by thirty they were gone from the upper deck, and by forty from the lower, and by fifty, unlike her clothes, they were too big for her, clamped with crude fixative on to her gums, and seasoning each morsel of food with the taste of glue.

Not that Amy particularly liked the taste of rock, but where she lived, the name of *her* town, Amy Evans' town, was written indelibly inside, and she crooned it out after every bite. Porthcawl, it sang, no matter how you bit it. Neither a lick nor a nibble, a champ nor chew, could disturb its proud di-syllable. Porthcawl, it sang, to the last bite. Half way through was long enough to confirm her whereabouts, and then she would cover the left half of the stick with her thumb, nibbling down on the right, so that only 'cawl' was visible. That was the sound she liked most. It was the sound of the gulls as they screeched their way over from Ogmore Bay. Their cry was an even greater surety than the stick of rock of where she lived. Porthcawl. It was more important to her than her name. Amy Evans was not much to shout about, let alone embed into a stick of rock, or shriek across a stretch of sea. A common name almost, especially in Wales where it could, and did, apply to anybody. There was another one in the infants' class at school, and one of the big girls in the building on the other side of the playground, the building her Mam said she wasn't clever enough for, one of those big and clever girls was said to answer to the same name. One day, Amy had caught sight of her, and had gasped at her beauty, more with gratitude than with wonder, for there was a mincing thirty-one and a half-inch bosom proof that being saddled with such a handle did not preclude beauty. But our Amy was never to reach even the doubtful standards of that nubile standard fourer. She retained all her life the squat nose of her childhood, stubbed on to her face like a plasticine afterthought, a chin too long for any practical purpose, and eyes so close together that it seemed the sole function of the bridge of her nose to keep them apart.

But she had a good nature, as everybody said, and has to say when faced with one who has palpably little else. But Amy's mother would moan that her daughter didn't even have that, but was a wilful child, given to sudden rages and tantrums, who spat with hatred at her elder brother, who ran screaming down to the beach in anger or in unison with the gulls. 'Cawl, cawl, cawl,' she would scream, and as the gulls settled on the rocks the tears would dry, and the sense of her own common Amy-Evans ugliness would recede, for she knew the gulls found her beautiful. There she sat as the birds cooed and the breeze from the sea blew into her face her share of the beauty that her brother had so liberally helped himself to. The gulls would wait for her to leave, and it was always the same, no matter how long she stayed, for they were real gentlemen, Amy knew, the only real gentlemen she was ever to meet in her life. And as she slouched back up the hill, gathering her ugliness with each step towards her mother's house, she knew that the gulls had taken off silently, and she never once looked back to check, 'cos if you couldn't trust gulls you couldn't trust anybody.

Then back to the house and in through the side door, creeping softly into the parlour where her horrid brother would be playing with his trains, and with luck with his back to the door. Then she would jump on him from behind, and see him go blue in the face from shock. Too blue for tears, too blue even for a whimper, and her mother would never know how once again she had tried and failed to frighten her brother to death.

It was the others who made her hate him. Her Mam and her Dad who petted and coddled him, the neighbours who brought him gifts, whispering pity behind their sieving fingers.

'Stan's a sickly child,' her Mam would often say, and she didn't know what it meant, but supposed that 'sickly child' meant brother. Whatever it was it irritated her, especially its tightly packed black curls, large liquid eyes, and its undeniable beauty, half of which at least was rightly hers.

'What's a sickly child?' she asked one day, at the end of her tether, her brother on her mother's knee. And her Mam had simply stretched across and slapped her face.

'Cawl, cawl, cawl,' she screamed down to the beach, where the gulls came to greet her and console.

When she was older she heard Dr Rhys say rickets, and she remembered that she had heard the word often and thought it was some kind of game. Now, what with the doctor there visiting Stan, the word belonged with little doubt to her brother.

'What's rickets?' she said one day, and dodging her Mam's outstretched and stinging palm she rushed again to the sea, crying, 'Cawl, cawl,' and when she reached the shore line she heard that her voice was crying alone, with barely an echo. No gulls came, or perched, or waited. 'Cawl?' she whispered, 'Cawl?' And as she climbed back up the hill, for the first time in her brief life she looked back at the sea, and the trust drained through her soul like the sand through her toes, as, with each step away from her rejection, she lost the heart of her childhood.

And that had been almost half a century since, hundreds of sticks of rock ago, and the gulls still came with their screeching, but now she rarely went to the beach. A woman has her pride; she does not expose her frailty. She sheds her tears alone. Fifty years ago, and the sickly child, now a sickly man, still with the thick curls, greying now, framing his pale imploring beauty. Stan Evans. Nothing special about his name, either, but they'd made it special, all of them, most now long since dead, but he thrived still on their love for him and special pleading. Stan had never needed a gull or a stick of rock. Porthcawl was his mere postal address, and if the gulls wanted to announce their arrival as his silly sister said, it was Stan Evans they would call from over Ogmore Bay, because Stan Evans was the only point in coming to Porthcawl in the first place. And now, as they lived abrasively side by side in their parents' house above the sands, the gulls would screech across the bay and Stan would turn a deaf ear, while Amy occasionally whispered 'Cawl,' for no matter how painful one's first rejection one cannot forever, except at the risk of one's own sanity, forgo the joy it once engendered.

* * *

As she sat by the table in the kitchen, mulling her veined hands, Amy wondered whether people could tell, no matter where they lived, that it was Sunday. In Porthcawl there were so many clues, even without the chapel bell, and the late milk, and the sudden musty smell of God. There were the gulls, who knew instinctively that Sunday, weather permitting, was a sure full house, and show-offs that they were, they gathered early and in great numbers, so that those countless day-trippers, those pigeon-fanciers from across the sea-less valley, could once and for all sort the men from the boys.

From about ten o'clock, the audience would filter in, setting up their plastic ware on the green, and a waft of meths would steam Amy's windows as they brewed up their tea. Vulgar, she thought. Not a bit like the old days, when you could look from the window across the green and down to the sea with nothing save an odd clump of gorse to disturb the line of vision. Now, by lunch-time, she would have to stand on a chair to see the sea, blocked almost by cars, tents and picnic paraphernalia. In the old days, Rest Bay, where they lived, was reachable only by car, so that only a handful of strangers, select and known to each other, would stake a sedate claim to a patch of green. And the tea came in thermoses with no smell, and the sandwiches were real chicken free-ranging on lettuce, and there were even serviettes that weren't made of paper. Her Mam hadn't minded them at all. They even added a holy touch of Sunday class, and her mother was not above nodding to them on her way down to the beach, but always with the proprietary right of an owner, murmuring almost, 'I hope you enjoy my sea.' Amy would hang about the cars, ambling from one to another, stepping on and off the running-boards, until her Mam would call her crossly, for it was so obvious from Amy's curiosity that the Evanses didn't have a car, and for a woman who owned the sea and the sand such an omission was unbelievable. Sometimes her Mam would let Stan stray into the circle of picnickers, so that they could stare and wonder at his beauty, and she would look at them and think, 'He's mine too.' But if Amy strayed into their circle, her Mam would pinch her stubby nose and guide her away from other's opinion, and Amy would hurry down to the sea, saying over and over again, 'Fuck, fuck', for though she had no idea of what it meant she knew that the word was terrible. Gwyneth Price, her friend at school, had said that if you ever said it you would go to hell, but Amy feared little for hell, sensing with little error that she was already in it.

'Those nice people up there from Cardiff,' her Mam would say when she reached the sands. 'They were actually using a silver teapot. Such a nice class of people.' And though Amy didn't know what 'snob' meant, any more than 'fuck', she knew that both in some way belonged to her mother.

Her Dad never went to the beach, not even in the old days when it was deserted and few would have seen him. He considered it undignified to frequent places where it was not required to dress formally. Even at home at breakfast on the weekend he appeared tied and collar-studded as for every working day. Once Amy had asked him what his job was, and he had answered as if she were a grown lady, 'I'm a solicitor's clerk,' and she knew better by this time than to ask what it meant, 'cos it might have come under the same filing system as 'rickets' and 'sickly child'.

'What's your Dad do then?' her friends would ask in school.

'He's a solicitor's clerk,' without flinching.

'What's that then, when the cows come home?' Gwyneth said.

'There's stupid you are,' she would say, and in such a way that they felt it with deep assurance, and deduced that Amy Evans' father did something so clever and so important that no one could understand it. Which is what Mr Evans would have wanted, because his driving ambition, fed by an overwhelming sense of self-importance, was to become Mayor of Porthcawl. At the time when Amy had stopped questioning, around her seventh year, he was already a Councillor, and she remembered how, when she was eleven, her birthday was actually celebrated for the first time, and she began to look at her mother with less bitterness, until she realised that it was not her celebration at all, but simply marked the day of her father's succession to aldermanship. She gathered that there was but one more step to take and, failing catastrophe, her father would don the Mayoral chain. She remembered little communication between her parents in those days, except for her Mam's constant admonition to her mayor-elect for to 'mind your elocution, Dai'. Another word.

'What's . . .' But she held her tongue.

As she grew up, Amy gleaned a lexicon of words without meaning, and later on in her life when, one by one, their meanings became clear, she was shipped right back to her tormented and silent childhood, and, as an antidote, she would whisper 'Cawl' softly to herself, for it was the only sound that could offset the pain of her recall.

'More dumplings, then, shall we, Stan?' her Mam would say, reaching Stan the bucket, and Amy would stand to one side and watch. She would wait patiently, crying inside herself for her mother's neglect. She waited until Stan and her Mam had achieved twenty

9

dumplings, her heart-ache mounting with the count. Then she took a long run towards them, and with growing joy in her heart she stomped over each dumpling, crushing each grain of Stan's painful effort and her Mam's hurtful partiality. Then she darted up the hill, passing the posh serviette people from Cardiff. 'Fuck, fuck,' she shouted at them. 'My Dad's going to be the fucking Mayor.'

And when Mrs Evans, a little later, carried Stan up the hill, she wondered why they didn't return her greeting and decided that the teapot was only Sheffield plate, and that they weren't so posh after all.

'I'll give you what for, my girl, spoiling our Stan's dumplings,' Mrs Evans shouted as she came into the kitchen. 'No jam for you today. Stan will have your share, won't you, my lovely.'

'I hope it makes him sick,' Amy said between blows. 'I hope he dies of it,' she added. Then, with her infinite courage, she turned to her Mam. 'You too,' she said, and it didn't matter what her mother did to her then. The relief of having it out, and saying it out loud, that she wanted her Mam to die, was so profound that it anaesthetised the pain of the blows.

'I'll let your Dad deal with you,' she heard her Mam say, but she didn't care what her Dad would do, or her Mam, because at that moment she had decided to leave home.

From where she sat at the kitchen table, Amy could see the ribbon road that she had taken, all seven years of her, the carrier bag cutting into her little fingers with all the weight of her own toothbrush and Stan's teddy bear. When the phrase 'leave home' had come to her, the image of a suitcase came with it. But she had no case, and she knew instinctively that to be taken seriously she had to take something apart from her own person. There was something final about a toothbrush, for this meant at least one night away, and her teddy bear too. But when she saw him lying on the bed, she loved him so deeply that she could not submit him to the perils of a nomad existence, so she took Stan's instead. That would show them. It took her some time to find a carrier bag, and then she saw it, in her mother's bedroom, full of knitting needles and wool. She emptied it quickly on to the floor, pulling the needles out of the cardigan her Mam was making for her Stan. She marvelled at how the stitches dropped, and she pulled the wool out across the floor until the garment was half its original length. That would teach them too. Then she packed the bag and slipped out of the garden door.

She knew that the road from the Bay into town was a long one. Once or twice she had been with her Mam and Stan on the bus, and they had counted six bus stops to the promenade. But she wasn't afraid, for it was light and sunny, and she skipped along pretending she was on an errand for her Mam. Some cars passed her, travelling back from the Bay, and in one of them she recognised the silver teapot picnickers. They stared after her through the back window of the car, and she put her fingers to her stubby nose at them, and shouted 'Fuck fuck,' under the noise of the engine. She skipped past the dairy farm, but she didn't take the short cut through the fields because she needed the company of a passing bus or car and the odd walker who occasionally made his way on foot to her Mam's beach and sea. And one of them was coming towards her now. She thought in the frame of her seven years that he was an old man, older even than her father. He stopped and waited for her to come towards him. Her foot trembled, but she could not turn back.

'Hullo, my lovely,' he said. 'Give you fourpence if you come in the fields.'

'What for?' she said.

'Fourpence to have a look at your pussy.'

She'd never heard the word before but instinctively she knew it wasn't her elbow he wanted a dekko of. 'You can have a look for a million pounds,' she said. Not that she thought she was worth that much—her mother had conditioned her to knowing her value as less than nothing—but that she knew that no one in the world could have a million pounds.

'You're a clever one,' he said.

'My Mam's coming on the next bus,' she panicked, seeing the bus stop not far from them. 'If you don't go away,' she squeaked, 'I'll tell our Mam on you.'

'I'll wait for your Mam then,' he said. 'P'raps she'll show me *her* pussy for fourpence.'

'Our Mam hasn't got a pussy,' she said with utter conviction.

He came towards her and she dodged, running down the ribbon road, while the back of her knees shot spasms of fear down to her ankles, and she didn't stop till she reached the promenade and the shops and the people.

'You in a hurry, missie?' a policeman stopped her.

'Got to catch up with my Mam,' she said, dodging past him.

How odd, she thought, that in the short seven-year span of her life, her mother had never come in so handy. She stopped at the pier, and sat on a bench to get her breath back. And for the first time, she realised that she had left home.

She took Stan's teddy bear out of the bag and tried to cuddle it on her lap. But she couldn't give it the love she would give to her own. Stan's bear was so clean, so unworn, so unhandled. Uncle Ivor had given them each a teddy bear last Christmas, but Amy's love-biting had worn hers to a frazzle. One ear was half-chewed and the other had lost all its stuffing so that it flopped over one eye, winking at her with the knowledge of what they both had to endure. She couldn't cuddle Stan's bear at all. She felt like its wicked stepmother, so she stuffed it back into the carrier bag and hoped that Stan was already crying for it. But it couldn't be his bedtime yet. Lots of children of her own size were playing up and down the pier still, and nobody shouted for them to come home to bed. She wondered why her Mam wasn't there looking for her, why the whole police force of Porthcawl, all twelve of them, were not scouring the pier and the beaches on the side. And then the thought struck her that her Mam was glad she had gone and hoped that she would never come back, and that she would keep her disappearance secret. For a moment Amy thought she'd go back home just to spite her. But she might meet the pussy-man on the way. Then she would never get home, ever again. She knew it wouldn't get dark for a long while, and she was glad it was summer. Surely they would start looking before dark came. She would see them first, all the policemen, and dogs, and perhaps, if she was lucky, her Mam tearing her hair behind and crying her heart out for all the horrible things she had done to her only daughter, and if only God would find her, she would love her ugly Amy all her life. Then Amy would hide, watching them at the search, gloating over her Mam's anguish, and after a while she would casually show herself. She would be caught by chance and reluctantly, and she would tell the whole of Porthcawl on her Mam, and she'd say 'fuck' too, in front of the policemen, so that her Mam would be ashamed.

She wondered how long it would take for anybody on earth to move a finger on her behalf. Again she thought of going home, and again of the pussy-man, and she wondered whether, when she grew up into a big lady, the choices in her life would be equally threadbare.

She started to cry, but she didn't want to draw attention to herself so she fumbled in the carrier bag and stared at Stan's bear with loathing. She heard a tuning-up from the end of the pier and she knew it was five o'clock. 'You can set your watch by them,' her Mam used to say, and for treats she would take her and Stan to the end of the pier to listen to the band. Now Amy would go on her own without anybody's permission or charity. She ran to the end of the pier and bagged a seat in the middle of the front row.

'Amy Evans,' one of the blowers called out from behind his tuba. 'What you doing there all on your own?'

'I'm waiting for our Mam,' she shouted back, which indeed she was.

'I'll have my eye on you,' he said with a wink, and Amy hated him 'cos he was always winking and blowing and minding everybody else's business. Even on his milkman's rounds, which was his regular job, he'd be winking and blowing and interfering. She waited for him to give a practice blow, and under the noise of it she shouted, 'I seen you put water in the milk.'

He smiled at her. 'What's that you said?'

'Nothing. Only singing I was.'

The conductor rapped the stand with his stick and the tuning tapered. Then they all raised their horns to their mouths and blew. She didn't know what the tune was called, but they always started off with it while such audience as they were able to muster straggled in.

Amy put her hands on the chair each side of her, so that the milkman could see she was expecting her Mam and no doubt Stan who was always with her. She was feeling better now. The music was safe, and she was glad in a way that Moelwyn the Milk had seen her. She wriggled inside the blasts from the horns, and the puffs from the piccolos, and she sniffed the sea air as the wind shuddered the awnings on the pier, the sounds and smells spelt out the magic letters, not of her name which was so secondary, but of her place, her real identity, Porthcawl.

The time passed quickly as one familiar tune followed another. And then came their finale, as recognisable as their signature tune and the players blew as if their cheeks would burst. She picked on the trumpeter directly in front of her, staring at him, willing him to look back at her. And when he did, in the middle of a mighty blow, she puffed out her cheeks, pursing her mouth and nodding her head to his rhythm. Once, long ago, it seemed—when you were a big lady, she wondered, was long ago as long ago as long ago seemed when you were a child?—she had managed with this manoeuvre to so unnerve a young novice trumpeter that he had spluttered and spat his way hopelessly and sadly disconnected, through the remainder of the piece. But the player she now tried to unsettle was an old-timer, and too innured to end-of-pier trickery from little boys and girls who thought they were so bloody clever. And during a short rest in his bar, he managed to stick his tongue out at Amy, and then return to his blowing as if nothing had disturbed him.

'Fuck, fuck,' she mouthed under the noise, hoping he couldn't lip read. When the last fanfare sounded, she got up and walked away, trying to hide her running, and pretending to look for her Mam in case Moelwyn the Milk was watching her.

Now the pier was emptying, and she wriggled her way into a cluster of people, not wanting to appear alone. The smell from the chip-stand at the end of the pier made her suddenly hungry and she wondered whether her Mam had really meant it about giving Stan her bit of jam. She wondered how long she could go without food and then she saw her starved-to-death body lying on the rocks in the morning, her hair tangled with seaweed, and the trumpet-blower being sorry he'd stuck out his tongue at her, and Moelwyn the Milk telling everybody on his rounds that she'd said she was waiting for her Mam. 'Keeping seats for them she was, for her Mam and her brother, the sickly one you know. Lovely girl, Amy. Not pretty you know, but a soul as good as gold. Her Mam's grieving something terrible.'

'What's the matter then, little girl?' a fat lady wiped Amy's cheek with a dirty hanky.

'I lost my Mam,' Amy said.

'Don't you worry now. We'll find her. Here, have a blow.'

She offered the rag to Amy's stubby nose, trying to get a grip on it, but Amy tore herself away and ran and ran to the end of the pier, jumping down to the shingle under the jetty to hide. She peeped through the log supports, waiting for the fat Samaritan to appear, look about, and give up the good fight, which that lady shortly did and with little struggle. Amy crept out from underneath the pier and made for the rocks. She could climb them blindfold, her feet knowing the holds by heart, and she skipped across to the centre of the shingle, a rock-free area, where Tommy the ventriloquist would come and she'd know it was seven o'clock.

She waited, heartened a little in the knowledge that

she had managed to run away from home for so long. 'I'm a brave little girl,' she said to herself, 'and I don't ever need to go home again. I'll get a job and I'll make ever so much money, and I'll give it to the best doctor in the world to make our Stan better.' If only there were just her and Stan at home, and she could look after him, and her Mam and her Dad gone away for ever, not dead, but nearly. Then she could have her Mam's cameo brooch.

She took out Stan's bear, but its frigid newness still offended her. She wished that Stan was naughty sometimes, so that they could gang up against the common enemy. 'Oh I wish I was pretty,' she cried aloud, and she put the bear back into the bag.

Now they started to come down to the shingle from the promenade, the holiday people from across the valley. She knew they weren't from Porthcawl because they didn't know the rocks by heart, and even their children crawled over them full of fear. They were overtaken by the brown locals, skipping over the rocks, their feet bare, rehearsed through many summers. They bagged the front end of the shingle. Amy moved cautiously towards them. She wanted to be close to Tommy, too, to watch the adam's apple in the man's throat moving up and down while Tommy was talking. She knew Tommy couldn't really talk, 'cos he was only a doll. She knew it was the man who held him who said all Tommy's lines, but she didn't want to believe it. She wanted to be like Stan who thought Tommy was real and had a real voice, and he wasn't interested in proving otherwise. Sometimes when she didn't see the apple moving, she thought her friend Gwyneth was a liar. Gwyneth Price knew everything. She'd told her about Tommy even before Amy'd ever seen him. Gwyneth was full of knowledge. She said that babies came out of ladies' bellies, would you believe, but Amy'd never believe that, not ever, 'cos 'how could they get there in the first place, Gwyneth Price?'

'Not telling,' Gwyneth said. 'It's rude.'

'You're a fibber then.'

'Suit yourself.'

So Amy didn't want to see the apple move. 'Cos then she would have to believe about the babies.

The audience was really big now, sitting on the rocks and shingle, and she knew that any moment Tommy's voice would come from nowhere telling them good evening and welcome like he always did, and then his rose china face would appear above a rock, and he'd be laughing and chatting away and making all kinds of jokes, and that was the part that Amy liked most, because even if the apple was moving up and down like a road drill you couldn't see it. And then the man would appear and Tommy would tell him to go away, 'cos he wanted the audience all to himself. But the man wanted to be a star, too, and he'd carry Tommy over the rocks to the clearing of shingle, and stand with his throat hanging over Amy, so she couldn't avoid the apple if she tried.

'Good evening all,' the man said.

'Good even—' Amy started.

'Don't answer him,' Tommy was saying and she felt it as a personal rebuke.

'Good evening,' she said again, on the man's side. The man smiled at her, and she beamed back at him believing totally and once and for all that Tommy was a separate person.

She felt a hand gripping her shoulders. She turned her head to look at it, to study it almost, and though she knew, almost blinded by her tears, whose it was, yet it seemed unfamiliar to her, for she had never been in a position to look at it so closely. It had always been a fleeting shape across her face with sting attached. Now she could see the colour of the sting, the red chapped fingers and white knuckle, the blue anger of the veins.

'You come with me, my girl,' and the grip wrenched her from the shingle and over the rocks to the promenade. Then she noticed that her Mam was wearing an apron, a terrible thing in the middle of Porthcawl town, and curlers in her hair as well, and oh my lovely God, thank You ever so, the tears streaming down her Mam's face with the relief of finding her, and the tears, the curlers and the apron spelt out in public the loud alphabet of her grief.

'I'm sorry, our Mam,' Amy said.

'I'll make you sorry. You tell that to your Dad and to the policemen. Scouring Porthcawl we have for you,' she said.

A police car was waiting at the kerb, and she could see her Dad crossing the road to the pier.

'We found her,' her Mam shouted.

Her Dad turned and she saw him smile. 'Naughty girl,' he said running towards her. 'Duw, your Mam's been worried terrible.'

'All over now,' the policeman said, lifting her into the car, and they drove back up the beach road, passing the pussy-man at the bus stop, his four hot pennies in his hand.

She sat up in bed cuddling her bear. She knew that this night her Mam would come as she never did before to say goodnight to her. She heard her on the stairs and the rattle of a tray. 'I saved you your jam,' she said, 'and I brought you a nice cup of hot cocoa. How's that?' she said putting it before her.

'I'm sorry about your knitting, Mam.'

'You'll wind the wool for me tomorrow.'

'Yes, Mam.'

They both tried not to look at each other. Then Amy saw her mother's hands taking away the tray, and she felt them around her holding her tight. Why, even a kiss on her neck and cheeks, and God and Porthcawl I love you so, on her stubby, squat, ugly nose.

'Don't you ever do that again my girl. What would your poor Mam do without you?'

That night Amy cuddled her bear without a single nibble, and in the morning she understood why Stan's bear was so whole.

* * *

Stan'll be wanting his tea, she thought. Never ask for it, he wouldn't. Wouldn't trouble anybody for himself. Sometimes she wished he would be more demanding, more difficult, a little less saint-like so that her constant irritation with him would have some cause. But he was no trouble. He just sat there, in his bed at night and in his chair during the day, glad to be taken for a walk, grateful for a chat, but never asking for either, patient and beautiful with it. What's more, and Amy said it aloud while she brewed the tea, 'He's dying.' Dr Rhys, the son of Rickets Rhys, had pronounced it years ago, and careful not to give a dead-line. But Amy knew it would not be long. His coughing was worse and some days he seemed to have lost all strength in his hands. She could not bear to look at him then, when she held his cup for him, spooning the tea through his lips. She could not bear his beauty nor the sadness in his eyes for causing such trouble.

'Stan,' she called down the hall, 'you ready for your tea, then?'

'Lovely,' she heard him say, and she prayed to God for anger to seek him out, to dwell in him even for a moment and to rage against the cruelty of his chair-ridden life. A small and fleeting fury that would fling the tea tray to the floor, a plaintive 'Why?' from the throat, anything but his saint-like resignation.

'There's good you are to me, Amy,' he said, seeing the sponge she'd made for him.' Better than our Mam's,' he said, taking a slice. This way he tried to please her and tried also to get her to talk of old times. That's what he liked most, to recall his beach days, his attempted rock-climbs, his dumplings and his hot and young summers. But Amy would deny him that. His childhood was hers, too, and it crowded her memory often enough, unwilled and unwanted. She was not deliberately going to recall it.

'I felt like a bit of sponge myself,' she said.

He wheeled his chair towards the window. 'Can tell it's Sunday,' he said. 'Can't hardly see the sea. Well, they'll be gone when the sun goes down. Then ours it'll be, Amy.'

He was enclosing her. She tried not to hear him. She feared sometimes that his gentleness, his patience, his sheer undemandingness was a tyranny, that he would subjugate her with kindness, enslave her with his martyrdom. He would have her in the chair with him, for what right had she to legs, ugly and veined that they were, but whole.

'D'you remember before there were caravans?' he said. The past was all he wanted to talk about. He knew his future and there was little enough of it. His present was unbearable. It was his pre-chair days that mattered to him now and it was those days that she would not give him.

'I'll take you out after tea,' she said, going to the door.

'It'll be quieter then. Look at the mess you made now,' she shouted at him, seeing how the sponge had dropped on the floor. 'All day I'm clearing up after you,' she said, picking the crumbs up one by one. 'Be more careful now.' She went quickly from the room before he could apologise, slamming the door on his meek regrets, trundling back to the kitchen, her hand clutching four crumbs. 'Oh Amy Evans,' she said to herself, 'how can you be so mean of spirit, so small of soul.' Wasn't it enough for her that he was bound to the chair, hating every move she had to make on his behalf. It was her house-pride that was corroding her. Stan was the only untidy spot in the whole house. Each room was spotless, and she would spring clean endlessly, open each door again and again through the day, viewing its spotlessness, and knowing that it was good. 'Your kitchen's clean enough, Amy, for to eat off the floor,' Gwyneth would say, and so it was if you were so inclined, but Stan shed crumbs like dandruff. Oh if only he would be still in his chair, forever still, without moving, an object, so that all she had to do every day was to dust him.

The gulls shrieked from the beach, seeing the trippers put up their tents. Their first curtain call. She would wait for the beach to empty, and then she would take Stan for a breather along the road they had started building the very day they had put Stan in his chair. 'Building it special for you, Stan my lovely,' her Mam said that day when Rickets Rhys had pronounced Stan non-ambulent. The old doctor had died only a few days afterwards, and Amy wasn't sorry, 'cos someone had to punish him for that chair. For some reason she thought that now old Rickets was gone he would have taken his diagnoses with him, and that once the old doctor was buried Stan would rise from his chair and run down to the beach faster than he'd ever run before. But she wasn't surprised when it didn't happen. Even as a child she didn't believe in miracles, and she knew that young Rhys Rickets would inherit not only his father's rounds but his verdicts too.

She manoeuvred the chair out on to the porch. 'Where shall we go then?' she said, though there was only one way, all others being over the sandy cliff where a chair walk was precarious. Though she'd often thought of trying it. 'It was an accident, m'lud. We were looking at the view, d'you see, and the chair slipped, and there he was, chair and all at the bottom of the cliff.'

'Let's go over to the car-park,' she said. 'It's empty now and we can look at the sea.' She swivelled the chair round and on to the green, looking for a car-less clearing with a view of the beach. She had to wheel Stan a good half mile before they found a space, and then she parked him, standing behind him still. She realised how rarely nowadays she looked at him, speaking to him obliquely or from behind, and when she could not avoid his face it was not only his beauty that she saw but her pilfered own.

'We used to picnic just about here,' Stan was saying. 'Remember?'

He was at it again. What was so great about his iron-legged childhood that he should wish so often to recall it, days when he would climb down the sand dunes on his bottom, and waddle down to the sea, a cherub in splints. Amy didn't answer. His past, laced with his Mam's sweet love, hurt her too much. She wished she could forgive it and all it had done to her. She had thought that when her mother died the bitterness would flag. But if anything its appetite increased.

23

Her father's death had made no difference, either; her hopes now lay undeniably with Stan. She sat down on the grass beside him.

'I'm not well, Amy,' he said. 'I shan't see the sea much more.'

She found herself looking at him, squarely into his beautiful face, and she felt a hole in her chest. She realised for the first time how desolate her life would be without him, how he would take away forever the past that shrouded her, and without which she could not survive. Alone, her ugliness would stare her back in the mirror, and there would be no other mirror to off-set it. She covered her horrid face with her hands and wondered how she would live without him.

'You've got a good few years yet, our Stan,' she said. 'Why, I might even go before you.'

A clutch of gulls flew over the waves below them. 'Cawl, cawl,' Amy heard them, as clearly as she had heard them all those sticks of rock ago. She clutched the handles of Stan's chair with its dying load, as the old childhood faith in the gulls returned, as it had to, for what would be left to her when the chair was empty? She turned and wheeled Stan back to their Mam's house as the gulls perched and waited. And she didn't look back, not once, 'cos she knew they would wait there until she had gone. Gentlemen, they were, gulls, especially those who homed in full cry towards Porthcawl.

A charabanc was taking off down the road with the last of the Sunday trippers. 'D'you remember the chara that took us to Dad's party, Amy?'

'Yes,' she said eagerly, for it was one of the few memories that re-awoke pleasure. But she didn't want to share it with Stan, any more than the pain, for both were private.

'I'm thinking about it,' she said.

'So am I, and by the time we've reached the house p'raps we'll have come to the end of the party. When we get there, Amy, will you tell me how far you are, or when you finish if it's quick?'

'I'll tell you then, our Stan,' she said. She wondered whether only dying people played races with memories. She would gladly dawdle over this one and be the loser. Stan had less time, and he'd be on to his next recollection and the next, Death his only competitor, until one day—not for a long time yet, please God—he would look over his shoulder and glimpse the end of an overtaking shadow, and she wondered what sweet memory of his would fall short of its full recollection.

'Finished!' Stan said as the house came into view. 'Remember the Co-op Camp? Remember?' Now for once he'd got her to play the game, he had to make the most of it. But Amy still dwelt in her first party, in her pretty dress, when all her ugly pieces were so much smaller. Eleven years she was, with small swellings on her chest which she stuck out till her back was strained and hollow. 'Put your chest in, you hussy,' her Mam would say, and then Amy'd round her shoulders like a hunch-back to spite her. The battle between them had never let up. After Amy had run away there was a truce, but it had not lasted long, and Amy's teddy bear once more bore the brunt of her anger. Every morning Stan would wake up and say, 'Are you Mayor yet, Dad?' and Dad and Mam would laugh like they never laughed with Amy. Then one day Dai Evans actually made it, and without elocution either, and he gave a party in the town hall for the children of Porthcawl.

She always took up the memory in the same place, when she was standing against a marble pillar on the dance floor, sticking out her two buttons and pretending to be fascinated by the chandelier. She would prolong this part of the memory, for what was to come was so exciting that it still had the power to stir her breasts, fallen now, and shrunken, unfelt for so many years that the nipples were unfindable.

'Want to dance, then, Amy?' Gareth put his arm in a crook and she placed her waist inside it, while every muscle in her body melted, and she knew that nobody on earth in all the history of man had known such feelings before. 'Look at me Gwyneth Price if you can bear it, 'cos who's dancing with Gareth Jones, and don't pretend now you're not jealous, 'cos every girl in Porthcawl's after him, and look who he's chosen, see?' He whirled her round and round, and so involved was she in the recollection that the rhythm wound itself round her bunioned feet, and Stan's chair rocked.

'Mind out, then,' Stan said good-humouredly, for he was in his memory too, not dancing like Amy, but ironclad with his mother's hand in his, and ice-cream with as much to come as he could eat, and balloons to burst and streamers to throw and a million joys that had nothing to do with mobility.

Amy danced on until the music was finished, and he asked her again and again, until she knew it was not out of pity. He danced her towards the stairs and down to the first landing where there was no one about. Amy went over that bit in her mind, down the stairs, to the landing where they leaned together over the balustrade and his fingers moved so gently over her farthing breasts.

'Finished!' Stan shouted. 'Finished with the party. Where are you up to then, Amy?'

She hated Stan then, for interrupting the only happiness she had ever known. 'Finished, too,' she said, struggling bitterly with the chair over the doorstep.

'That was a nice walk, Amy,' he said. He took the evening paper out of the letterbox as she wheeled the chair through the door. 'I'll read it in the kitchen,' he said, 'and watch you getting our supper.' He sensed her irritation. 'Or shall I be in the way?'

'Of course not,' she grunted. 'How could you be in the way?'

He let it pass. She might even, in her twisted and sad way, have meant it as a compliment, so he let her wheel him into the kitchen and place him beside the table where he could spread his paper. She peeled the potatoes. No more memories. Just the present, the interminable monotonous present, and the threat that forever lay over her of being utterly on her own.

'Would you like a potato pie, Stan?' she said, knowing it was a treat.

'You're good to me, Amy,' was what he said and what she expected, so that she could have chorused it with him. But she wasn't good to him, she knew, whatever he said. She wasn't good to him because she couldn't love him, as her Mam could never love her. Did one ever learn to love, she wondered. Anybody? She had loved Gareth, if that was what it was, though it was too short-lived to be absolutely sure, and she was back on the landing again where Stan had interrupted her. But her appetite for that memory sickened, for afterwards there had been nothing but a cold indifference. For on the day after the party, when she and Gwyneth were walking home from school, Gareth passed them on his bike, staring right through her scarlet blushing and her stuck-out hillocks as if his fingers had never strayed there, not ever, nowhere near, and never likely

27

to, thank you very much. And her best friend Gwyneth didn't even try to hide her satisfaction.

She grated the onions into the pie, and let the tears fall.

'Why did you say that then,' she asked Stan gruffly, 'about not seeing the sea much more? That's no way for to talk. Dr Rhys said you were much better. Don't want you brooding now.'

'I didn't want to upset you, our Amy,' he said. 'Only when I see the sea, d'you see, I think it's so beautiful, it cannot last. The sea, I mean, and I know that's daft, so it must be me after all that'll go. But I'll be here for some time yet,' he said laughing, and when the laughter dissolved into a racking cough Amy knew that that time was not long. She patted him gently on the back, and reached to the mantlepiece for his medicine. He took a spoonful gratefully and the cough subsided. He smiled. 'What's in the papers?' she said quickly, avoiding his gratitude yet again.

"There's been a bank robbery in Cardiff,' he said. 'St Mary's Street. That's by the station, isn't it? Haven't been to Cardiff for years.'

'How much did they take then?'

'Thirty thousand. Oh what would you and me do with that?'

'Take you on a cruise, Stan,' she said, 'so you'd see the sea night and day and nothing else. That'd make you sick of it.'

'Never,' he said. 'Where would we go then, Amy?'

'To America,' she said, entering the game. It was a new one with them and it promised more than memory-racing, because it had nothing to do with anything that had or would ever in a lifetime happen. It was safe, and nobody's fault.

Stan set out on his cruise leaving Amy to make her

own way. For suddenly he could walk, run even, up the gangplank and into the suite of rooms reserved for him. Amy would be further down the corridor so he could keep an eye on her if she got lonely. He unpacked and changed quickly into his bathing trunks. Then he lay on the floor for his exercise routine. He stretched first his right and then his left leg, one after the other, gaining in speed until he had reached a bicycling movement. He felt the stretch in his legs from thigh to toe, tingling with health and vigour. Then he reached for his robe and rushed up the stairs to find the pool. The liner was drawing away from the dock and he could see the white cliffs of Dover drifting by, but maybe it wasn't Dover if they were going to America like Amy said, but he loved the cliffs, so France would have to do. Yes, here was the sea in plenty and he would never tire of it. He fixed his eye on a white spittle-lick of wave and followed it as it broke towards the ship and sprayed into air against the bows. Then another wave and another. He felt the stretch of his limbs again, the flexibility in the knee, the suppleness of the ankle, the mobility of the toes. This was all in a lifetime he ever wanted. Amy could dream what she wished and as long as she wanted, for Stan could bask in the wholeness of his body and the salt tang of the sea for ever.

Amy leaned over the rail. The spray from the under-tow caught her face and she wiped her hand over it. Gently she caressed the nose, aquiline now, and noble, and then the large startled eyes and gentle chin. She heard a footstep behind her, and she knew from her reading of *The Lady's Companion* that a gentleman stood by her side, and that soon he would ask her name, and later they would dance, and by the end of the voyage he would have asked her for her hand, and only then would he confess to her that he was a lord of the realm. She knew what he looked like from the picture of the centre spread, which had also given her a clue as to her own image, though most of her face lay snuggled on his chest. A few gulls settled on the bridge of the ship, but she had no wish to say 'Cawl', because she was Amy Evans no longer. She was, if she remembered rightly, Jacintha Somers, and who needed gulls with such a name. But as the ship's hooter sounded, she remembered that she'd left Stan alone and she was back in the kitchen getting his supper, while he sat strapped in his chair, looking at his sea.

'Supper,' she shouted at him, reckoning too much dreaming wasn't good for him, and he jumped back into the terrible truth of his stunned limbs. She put a plate before him and they ate in silence. He said he would make an early night. He wanted to be alone, to go back to his sea again, lying on his cabin bed in natural and wholesome lay-out, following the movement of the waves through the porthole.

When Amy had cleared away, she sat down and read the evening paper. For her there was no point in going back to the ship's rail. No matter how strong the reality of her dreams, the solid truth of Stan's wheelchair was stronger. If he were dead, she thought, could she then dream in freedom, with nothing on earth to bring her back from her fancied beauty, her reverie loves and loving. The thought that one day she might find herself alone horrified her. There would only be the cleaning left once Stan had gone, and who would make the house dirty for her to clean it again? Quickly she opened the newspaper to take her mind off such terrible thoughts. She found the item of the bank robbery that had sent them both a-voyaging. 'Two-armed men,' she read. Disgusting, she thought, not bothering to read further. A father was imprisoned for beating his child. Disgusting too, as was the middle spread of a bathing beauty exposing herself on a rock. But most disgusting of all was to be found in the Personal Column which Amy read, salivating. 'Young widower wishes to meet lady.' 'Divorced gentleman seeks companion, etc.' And then, bold as brass, 'Middle-aged lady seeks gentleman, view matrimony.'

Disgust almost exploded inside her. She read the little notice over and over again, her bile mounting. Amy Evans did not know what the world was coming to, and she half feared, and more than hoped, that she too could be swept along by the filthy tide that engulfed it.

*　　*　　*

'That's the doorbell,' Stan called out, as if Amy couldn't hear it though its chimes rang through the house like a stern call to prayer. Amy's Dad had the bell installed when he'd clambered into mayoral office. It was the first of its kind in Porthcawl, and Amy used to stand outside the door pressing the button of the four long minims over and over and over again, until her Mam would scream with Amy-anger.

Amy would laugh, for what her Mam had boasted was a status symbol now seemed the means of driving her mad.

'That'll be Gwyneth,' Stan shouted again, though that too was a foregone conclusion, for Gwyneth Price came every morning and usually at the same time.

'She'll be bringing the bread,' Stan finished.

Amy knew that too, and she wondered whether every morning Stan repeated his chorus just to annoy her, or whether perhaps he simply wanted to remind her that he was still there.

'Coming, Gwyneth,' she shouted through the last minim.

Gwyneth held the bread before her, its crust jutting out of the end of the bag. It was still warm.

'I can smell it,' Stan shouted as Gwyneth came in through the door.

'Don't be greedy now,' Gwyneth said, as she did every morning.

'It'll be nice with a bit of home-made jam,' Amy said, for it was her turn. It wearied her, this tired repetitive matutinal dialogue, its cheerfulness more and more forced each morning. Gwyneth put the bread on the kitchen table and looked around her. Amy waited for her to say her line.

'It's so clean your kitchen, Amy, you can eat off the floor.'

Had she been on cue, Amy would have smiled as she did every morning and shrugged off the compliment. But suddenly she craved some change, so she said nothing, turning her back to the sink.

'You can eat off your floor,' Gwyneth tried again.

Amy swung round at her, unsmiling. 'Prove it,' she said. For Gwyneth Price had never proved anything. She knew all the facts, of course, did Gwyneth. She it was who had told Amy where babies came from, but the burden of proof lay on others. She knew, too, how they got there, but she had even less proof of that. Gwyneth Intacta Price, and proud of it she was, and slightly disgusted with those who were otherwise. Though they were the best of friends, Amy felt slightly superior to Gwyneth. For Amy had proved it. Gwyneth may have had the facts of the equation, but Amy had provided the Q.E.D. Certainly of how babies got there in the first place.

The method had been painful, she remembered, and

in her single and sad experience, infallible. 'Oh it can't be,' she had moaned inside herself, wondering whom to tell, and terrified of telling anybody. Once more and for the hundredth time she read the section from the book of Home Medicine that her Dad had bought with his cigarette coupons. 'The signs,' it said. Omens, more likely. 'Stopping of periods,' and she hadn't had one for two months, and her breasts were painful like it said in the book. Another week or two and she'd be sick in the mornings. Two hundred and eighty days, it promised her, from the time of conception, and so single was her experience she could have guaranteed delivery date with certitude. It was that fact that pained her most of all. Surely other pregnant women couldn't tell with such assurance. But for her there was only one time, and no more, either before or since. Gwyneth had said that doing it was lovely, ever so, so lovely you couldn't explain it. Well, it was the only fact that know-all Gwyneth got wrong, for Amy remembered only three sharp stabs of pain, and then it was over. Then he'd got up from the ground, buttoning, and left her lying behind the maintenance shed of his barracks.

'Parlee Voo,' she called after him, for that was the only name she knew him by. That's what she and Gwyneth called the Free French stationed in Porthcawl. 'Parlee Voo?' she whispered again, seeing the blood on her knickers that he had torn across her thigh. He had disappeared into the dark. She wiped her eyes and tidied herself as best she could. She knew even without a mirror that she looked suddenly different. Gwyneth would notice it straight away when she got to the canteen where they both worked. Night shift it was for them this week, and she was already late. She hobbled across the parade ground, glad that it was dark, but she stumbled and fell, and remembered that she had left her torch behind the shed. She couldn't go back for it; she never wanted to see the place again, so she had to grope her way in the black-out. She knew that the entrance to the canteen was opposite the main barracks, and she caught the silhouette of the building not far in front of her. She walked away from it until she heard canteen noises and was able to make her way towards them.

Gwyneth was filling the urn. 'You look like you've come through a hedge,' she said.

'I forgot my torch,' Amy said. 'I fell over a flagstone.'

'Fancy coming without your torch,' Gwyneth said. 'Haven't you heard there's a war on? You feel all right, Amy?' she went on. 'You look white as a sheet.'

'I'm OK,' Amy said. 'Just been running.' She fiddled with the cups and saucers wondering whether out of the dozens of Free French who that evening would queue for their cups of tea, she would recognise the particular Parlee Voo who had deflowered her. She doubted it and she knew that it was irrelevant. A few minutes ago she had had proof of the lesson her Mam had diligently taught her; that all men were the same, and that all were hateful. It didn't occur to her that she was pregnant. Some women she knew, married and respectable, tried for years for a baby. It was a hit and miss affair. Even Dad's Home Medicine admitted that, so when the time for her first period came and went, she idly looked that one up in the book too, and found it ascribable to emotional upset. Well, she'd had that all right, so she wasn't unduly disturbed, but when the second moon waxed and waned bloodless, she tremblingly opened the book again, at the section she'd taken care to avoid, and her symptoms were there in cold print, as if she'd dictated them herself. She counted on her fingers. She was in her forty-fifth day of gestation. In the page of illustrations that followed, she found a picture of the foetus approximating to her time, and she felt suddenly sick. She didn't want that hideous growth inside her; she had to get rid of it, and quickly too. But she couldn't do it on her own. She'd heard of do-it-yourself women who had ended up on mortuary slabs. And though she'd never seen much point in living, she didn't yet want to die. She'd heard of the gin method. A whole bottle neat, and a hot bath with mustard in it. But where in one-eyed Porthcawl, and in the middle of a war, could she get a bottle of gin. Over Rest Bay, in the American Forces camp, there was gin in plenty, she'd heard, and plenty of GI's who would give you anything for a feel, and even nylons for a bit more. Well, she had nothing to lose.

She crept out of the house—even at twenty, her Mam insisted on knowing her comings and goings—and she directed her torch towards the American camp. She had to walk over the sand dunes, for the beach was fenced with barbed wire. As she neared the perimeter of the camp she heard laughter and singing. She held the noise in the beam of her torch and moved towards it. A group of soldiers stood at the door of the canteen, about a dozen as she made out, sharing two girls between them. She moved to within a distance of a few yards, and then stood still, weaving her torch in an arc around her.

'Looking for me, honey?' a voice came through the darkness.

And then another. 'Come on over, baby, and let's have a look at you.' She froze where she stood. She hadn't reckoned on that. She had come prepared to give them a feel in the black-out, and a bit more if that was the going price for a bottle of gin, but not to be examined in the cruel light of their torches. She wanted to run away, but they were already coming towards her. Two of them, a second opinion.

'Hi, baby,' one of them said, taking her hand and the torch with it. He shone it brutally into her face, and they spoke their opinion aloud. In unison they gave a low and long whistle, which she and they knew as a cat-call, and they turned away laughing, throwing the torch at her feet. She felt a sudden gratitude for Parley Voo, who, in spite of the trouble he had caused her, had found her terrible face no obstacle. With one hand she picked up the torch and held her fretting stomach with the other. She pitied it, this stomach of hers, as if it didn't belong to her, that it was so uncared for and so unloved. But as she walked along the sand dunes the pity turned to hate, and she stood and stared down at herself, tearing her thighs apart, and screaming into the wind, 'Bleed, you bugger, bleed.' Then she sat down on a mound, ripping the grass from the sand. By the light of the half moon, she could see the black shadows of the hovering gulls on the water. If she strained her eyes, she could hear their cry. Their 'cawl' was almost a whisper, as if, in token of their war effort, they were observing an aural blackout. No German bomber pilot would ascertain his whereabouts from their cry. So she whispered to them, too, for she had to tell somebody. 'I'm in trouble,' she said to the sky. 'I'm in the family way.' It was out, on the wind, the terrible knowledge that at last she could share, and she cried with the relief of it. She cried all the way home, and as she reached her house, she saw her Mam's dreadful shadow in the doorway, scanning the entrance with her torch. 'Where have you been then, you dirty stop-out?' she shouted into the darkness. In the hall, her Mam saw her tear-stained face and, softening, she touched Amy's arm. 'What's the matter then, Amy love?'

And taking advantage of this brief affection, Amy looked into her Mam's face and said, 'Mam, I'm in the family way.'

Her mother took a step back and stared at her. A hot and red anger flushed across her face, and her cheeks filled with gathering vocabulary. She tightened her jaw, holding in all the words that she couldn't find enough words for, and she slapped Amy across her offending belly. Then she let the words out like a stream of fire.

'If you ever tell our Stan I'll break your neck,' she said. Then, sitting down in an effort to contain her spleen, she exploded with, 'And your poor Dad an Alderman.'

Amy stared at her. She was more horrified at her mother's reaction than at her own condition though, when she thought about it later on, it was entirely predictable.

'Well, you'll do it on your own, my girl,' her Mam was saying. 'I don't suppose you even know who the rotten father is, the way you gallivant, the hussy you are. Who was it?' she screamed at her.

'I don't know, our Mam,' Amy said, brazen, and for some reason feeling much better. 'Could have been one of about six.' She wouldn't give her mother the pleasure of knowing that her ugly daughter had no possibility of choice.

'You wait till I tell your Dad. Dad,' she shouted, still from her sitting position, as if, were she to rise, her insides would splutter out in anger. 'Your little prostitute's in the family way.'

Her Dad came to the door of the kitchen and looked at them both helplessly. 'Come inside,' he said to them. 'We'll have it out quiet.'

In the kitchen her Dad sat and said nothing, while

her Mam cried loud and full of snot. Amy had the feeling that none of what was going on had anything to do with her. She heard her Mam scream that she had to get rid of it, and she wondered what the 'it' was that she was supposed to get rid of. Then at last, her Dad spoke. 'D'you want it, Amy?' he said quietly.

It was enough for her that he had asked. 'No,' she said, looking straight at him.

'Then I'll see to it,' he said.

He arranged for her to go to Cardiff. There was a lady doctor there, a refugee from Germany. His friend on the Council knew her. She owed him a favour, but for what he did not specify. Amy's Dad went to Cardiff himself to look the lady over, to ascertain that it wasn't a knitting needle procedure, and having satisfied himself he paid half on deposit. He hardly spoke a word and the doctor could see the lump jumping in his throat. She put her hand on his arm.

'Look after my little girl, Doctor,' he said.

They were dropping bombs on Cardiff every night, and it didn't help that the doctor lived in the dockland area. 'It's part of the risk,' her Mam said, as she saw Amy off on the red-line bus. 'Don't say you didn't ask for it.'

'Come with me, Mam.'

Her mother wiggled her nose at the din of the traffic, and Amy saw how she pretended not to hear her plea.

The bus was full but as it neared Cardiff it emptied noticeably. You didn't go to Cardiff in the dark unless you had special business there. And it was almost dark, four o'clock in the winter, dark enough for bombs and for fear. But it was not the bombs that frightened her.

'There's nothing you can do about it,' her Mam would say, not even bothering to go to the shelter. 'If the bomb's got your name on it, well it's yours. That's a fact.' And as Amy walked from the bus stop down the docks road, she almost hoped for a bomb with her name on it loud and clear, not Porthcawl this time, but Amy Evans, that name that was never for living but suitable only in large capitals for her tomb. Yes, a bomb right now, she thought, would come in nice and handy, would absolve her from walking one step further towards what she knew would be murder. She tried to think of what was inside her as a growth, sprung from a nature not of her making, a growth that, like any other, must be cut out. She held her hand on her belly, stroking it tenderly. 'Poor little parlee voo,' she whispered, and she prayed for a bomb to fall. She leaned against the railings, and as she stood there the sirens began to wail. She smiled, watching the few people on the street scurry past. Even a cat, mean with every one of its lives, jumped down from the railings where she stood and scented its way home. By the time the sirens had waned she was alone in the street, with searchlights sweeping across the sky and the distant grunt of guns.

'Get inside,' a voice called out to her. She was caught in the beam of a torch, and she heard angry running steps. She did not see the ARP Warden until he was almost on top of her. 'Get inside somewhere,' he shouted at her, more angry at her stupidity than concerned for her safety. She ran away from him, her torch in one hand and the other still sitting gently on her stomach. She slunk along the pavement as fast as the light would allow. The guns were louder now and she could hear the distant drone of the planes. She reached the waterfront and the steps down to the landing stage. She was surprised that no one was about. She thought that someone should be on sentry duty at such an obvious target. She was glad though, for she was able to run down the steps and sit on the flagstones and look at the black water criss-crossed with searchlight beams. It was quiet now. The guns were distant again and she heard no planes. Perhaps they were on their way to Swansea, and they would have to pass over Rest Bay to get there. She uttered a feeble prayer for a premature dropping on to the American barracks and their whole rotten consignment of gin, and that the consequent blast would blow the parlee voos back where they came from. 'But spare our Mam and our Dad and our Stan,' she heard herself saying.

It was silent now. Even the guns had stopped. The searchlights were switched off and it was black everywhere. The water made no sound. No lapping here or waves, but she knew the water was there by the sheer silence of it. 'Cawl?' she whispered. 'Cawl?' In answer the guns broke out again with loud roaring. She saw a sudden fire in the sky and then a stream of flame dived into nowhere. She heard the dropping of bombs, four in a row, rhythmically timed, like the minims on their doorbell back home. The sky was lit by a red glow, close by it seemed, where the town centre was. She got up and walked up the steps to the dock road. She wondered for a moment what she was doing there with her hand glued to her belly. Then, with sickness in her heart, she remembered. She directed her torch on to the house numbers until she found 84. She took her hand off her stomach in a gesture of farewell and pressed the bell.

Dr Weiner opened the door herself, only slightly so as not to let out the light, and Amy squeezed herself into the hall.

'You are late,' the doctor said gruffly.

Amy put her hand back on her belly. It wasn't too late, she thought. She could still go away to some unknown place and drop it out of her. But the doctor, with a firm grasp on Amy's arm, was ushering her into a back room.

'Have you by you the remainder of the money?' she said.

Amy took the envelope out of her bag and passed it over without a word.

'Take off the clothes,' the doctor said. 'There by the door is a gown.'

She did not go out of the room, but turned her back discreetly. Amy wondered why she bothered with such a small act of discretion. In a few moments she would be naked, both in and out, and at her disposal.

'You can look if you like,' Amy shouted with all her fearful anger, baring her naked breasts to the doctor's back. 'I don't give a fuck.'

'That I am knowing already,' the doctor said, thinking inside herself that she was very clever. She turned around as Amy was buttoning the gown.

'Lie on the table,' she said. 'Can you climb up?' But her words were lost in a tremendous bang, and the house shook with terror, and the row of metal instruments on the side table shuddered.

'A bomb,' the doctor said superfluously. Then another fell, and another, and on the fourth, the window of the room shattered behind the black-out curtain. The doctor showed no signs of fear as she helped Amy on to the table, but Amy was trembling.

'Don't be afraid,' Dr Weiner said, her voice suddenly gentle. 'It will soon be over.'

Amy wasn't sure what she was referring to, but whatever it was she wanted nothing to do with it.

'I want to go back home,' she said.

The doctor started to speak again, or so Amy could see by her mouthings, but her voice was drowned in yet another dropping, this time so near and so loud that it seemed to have fallen on the house itself. When the rumblings had subsided the doctor tried again. 'Now, my dear,' she said, 'I am putting a little something in the arm. When I say it, you will count to ten. You understand?'

Amy stared at her face with terror, not wanting to see the needle go into her arm. She was convinced the doctor was a murderer and she was none too sure whose life she was taking.

'Now you count,' the doctor said.

'One,' Amy began, 'two,' and then reluctantly, 'three.' Her 'four' was drowned by another blast. She had a swift recollection of sitting on the rocks as a child and counting for ever and ever, because she knew that at some time she would reach a point when she could go no further. There was a last and final number in the world, and if she sat on the rocks long enough she would reach it, and know that there were no more. Now she knew that the last number in the Universe was a mere five, and after that there was no starting again. God punished you into nothingness for discovering His divine Code. It was a nothingness without dreaming, more nothing than a fluttering coma; it was the threshold of Death itself. And she welcomed it.

When she woke it was light. She did not recognise where she was. She was in a bed, and facing her was a large window, or rather, a large frame, for the glass was shattered on the floor. It was cold, with half the room open to the winter morning, so she snuggled under the blanket wondering where she was and how she came to be there. 'Six, seven, eight, nine, ten,' she heard herself saying, and then she realised what she had allowed to be done to her. Out of the sky came the All Clear siren, as the doctor opened the door with her breakfast on a tray. 'It's all over,' the doctor said. 'There was a bomb the next door after the next. Oh the mess from those Germans.' She put the tray on the bed-cover. 'Eat,' she said, 'you are better now.'

'Is it gone?' Amy said.

Dr Weiner nodded smiling. 'The next time,' she said, 'you must be married with the husband.'

'Never again,' Amy said, and she meant it fervently at the time, though she was not to know that never again would she have the opportunity.

She hadn't told Gwyneth the story, and if Stan knew he certainly had never mentioned it. It gave her a little self-status however, as far as Gwyneth was concerned, who comfortably considered her friend as one of her own kind, pure in heart and elsewhere, tight as a bloody drum in their bloomers, and talcum powder in their navels on a Sunday. She looked over at Gwyneth with infinite pity. Alone she was, with not even a Stan for company, keeping her dead Dad's bakery down the road. Not much custom now, what with the super-market on the corner, but there were still those that liked a home-baked loaf, unwrapped and touched by floured hands. Every morning Gwyneth would leave an assistant looking after the shop and she'd bring a fresh loaf to Amy and have breakfast with her friend and Stan. They were her only company. Now she was cut-ting her own baked bread, and it squashed with fresh-ness under the knife. You could smell it through the kitchen and out into the hall and Stan's room as he opened his door to wheel himself in to breakfast.

'Morning, Gwyneth,' he said, placing his chair near the bread board.

'Wait now,' Gwyneth said, 'till I've laid the table nice and tidy. You finished with the evening paper, Amy?' she asked, taking it off the table.

'Don't throw it away,' Amy said.

'What's so special then about last night's *Echo*?' Gwyneth asked, scanning the pages.

'I get a bit of fun from reading that column at the back. Disgusting it is,' Amy said.

'You don't want to be reading that rubbish, my girl,' Gwyneth said. 'Where is it, anyway?' She found the column and read it aloud. 'Widower, fifties, very lively. Fond of music and chapel, wishes to meet lady similar. View matrimony.' 'Oh, there's disgusting,' Gwyneth said. 'Marriages are made in heaven, not in newspapers. Isn't that right, Stan?' Stan didn't answer. You didn't argue with Gwyneth. She knew everything.

Gwyneth screwed the paper into a ball, wringing it with anger. 'Disgusting,' she spat, wringing it tight again. And then when no more filth could come out, she dropped it exhausted into the basket. 'Disgusting,' she almost screamed. It was the nearest Gwyneth Intacta Price would ever come to an orgasm.

When she had gone, and the breakfast and Stan cleared away, Amy reached into the wastepaper basket and ironed out the paper. She read the advertisements again. Yes, they were disgusting like Gwyneth said. But there was no need to throw the paper away. Waste, that's what it was. She folded it up and put it on the wireless. You never knew. A bit of newspaper always came in handy.

The gulls screeched into her sleep, and she woke, shaking off the tail-end of her terrible dreams. Through her window she could see flocks of them, diving and floating with cries of celebration. She hadn't thought of them for months and if they were there she hadn't noticed them. Their sudden arrival heralded the beginning of the spring season, the opening of the beaches, the boating pools and the fair. And the sun had come with them, blazing a harsh cold light on the unpicked sands. For no reason she knew she was glad of it, glad for another season and the return of the gulls. She even dared to whisper 'Cawl', that luke-warm talisman of her childhood. It embarrassed her a little and she giggled at her own nostalgia. She would give Stan a treat today, she decided. She would hire a taxi, fold up his chair, and take him to the fair.

She had laid breakfast before Gwyneth arrived with the bread, and Stan was up too with the sun and the gulls. She heard his chair creaking towards the kitchen. She saw Gwyneth coming up the path and was able to go straight to the door to let her in and thus avoid at least the beginnings of their monotonous morning dialogue.

'There's early everyone is,' Gwyneth said unwrapping the bread. 'Must be the first day of spring.'

'And a lovely day it is, too,' Stan said.

'It's still a bit nippy,' Gwyneth warned, 'so if you're going out, mind you wrap yourself up.'

Amy marvelled at all the new words, all the new lines that the characters had found for the opening of the new season. She joined in gladly. 'Thought me and Stan'd go to the fair today,' she said.

'Oh, that'll be a treat for you, won't it, Stan?' Gwyneth said.

Why did Gwyneth treat him like a child, Amy thought, and realised that she too babied him with her talk. But he had never taken exception to it as he had never complained about anything. She was wrong to diminish him so, and she resolved in this new season to speak to him as if he were not in a chair, as if he did not need sometimes to be fed and to be washed, as if indeed he were her elder brother and not some flagging foundling her Mam had bequeathed her. 'I'll hire a taxi, Stan,' she said primly. 'So we can fold up the chair.'

'There's good you are to me, Amy,' he said, and she stifled her first cry of the new season. The sun wasn't enough, nor the gathering gulls, nor the varying dialogue of morning encounters, nothing would ever be enough to balance the overweighted scales between herself and Stan's wheel-chair.

Gwyneth was cutting the bread. 'I can smell it,' Stan said.

'Don't be greedy now,' Amy said automatically. 'It'll be nice with a bit of home-made jam.' She heard the hollow of the old performance, and she couldn't go on that way.

'I'll grow my hair, I think,' she said, out of nowhere and with no relevance.

Gwyneth was too embarrassed to comment, and Stan was silent to business not his own.

'Look nice, it will, long,' Amy pursued. 'Perhaps I'll have a perm.' There was no going back now, and Gwyneth thought her friend had taken a turn with spring fever. 'Might even buy myself a pair of trousers,' Amy tortured herself. 'They're all the rage now.'

Stan laughed. He couldn't help it, and Gwyneth feared again for her friend's sanity. Amy turned on Stan and would have shouted at his mockery, but she knew that the only way to save herself now was to pretend that it had all been a joke, and she joined in their laughter.

'Trousers,' Gwyneth said with relief. 'Disgusting.'

It was an overworked word, and considering she and Amy shared it equally, it was a wonder it had not lost all its meaning. But both Amy and Gwyneth were able to pronounce it with such venom and such spleen, and they had ample supply of both, that the word from their lips could have done overtime for ever without losing one iota of its rage. And so they breakfasted together as they did every morning, and would do, Amy knew, for the rest of their natural lives, now the three of them, and then, with a shudder, two, and one there would be who would breakfast alone, and she prayed inside herself that it wouldn't be she.

The taxi came at eleven o'clock, with the gulls shrieking a send-off. Stan's excitement was silent, and Amy was relieved that he spared her his continuous gratitude. Though it was indeed a treat for him, or whatever baby-talk one chose to use. He rarely went beyond the confines of Rest Bay, and since he had lived there all his life, in his pre-chair and iron-leg days, his experience was contained in the sea's horizon and sand dunes of the bay. Amy wondered why he was never bored. He seemed to enjoy being alone and rarely craved her company in the house. It was only when she took him into the sea's view that he wooed her for memory sharing. But at home, in his room, he was happy with his stamp collection, his books about ships and adventures at sea. Amy only had the cleaning and the caring of him, and once again she trembled at the thought of being left alone. 'Feeling fine, today?' she said to him. He nodded, smiling. She understood why she treated him as a child. That was the way he responded. That was how he always wanted it. Adult responses belonged to walking and to running. His immobility prompted his childlike behaviour. She ruffled his curly grey hair—she rarely touched him—and he responded with almost a gurgle of joy. At Coney Beach the taxi-driver off-loaded the chair and carried Stan out of the back of the cab.

'Going for a treat, then?' he said. He babied him as automatically as he would have shouted at a foreigner, for both in his eyes were retarded. She thanked him and wheeled the chair towards the fair-ground.

Porthcawl still boasted a steam fair, with a few side-shows propelled only by the barkers' cries and the trippers' gullibility. The centre-piece was a large merry-go-round, with the same horses and lions that Stan and Amy had ridden on as children. There was a large towering mat, and a children's boating pool. Much of the fairground was devoted to side-shows; ladies with snakes, fortune-tellers and shooting-galleries.

'You going on the roundabout, Amy?' Stan said. If she would not talk to him about their childhood, she could at least go up and down on a merry-go-round horse, and show it to him.

'Will you be all right, Stan?' she said.

He was delighted that she had acquiesced so readily. They waited for the roundabout to stop, then she chose a horse in front of Stan's chair. He waved to her as the organ music ground to its full volume, and he waited patiently until she would come round again. Meanwhile, and till the end of her ride, he would travel back into his sandy days, shrimping in the pools, crawling on the rocks, and hurtling iron-clad down the dunes.

But for the first time in his chair-pent days he could not travel back. He panicked. Had he lost the magic for ever? How now could he live out his life chaired to his confining present. The organ music was the same to which his merry-go-round lion had danced in his childhood. Even the ticket collector was the same, old Dai the Punch, hobbling from one horse to another. But neither the music nor old Dai helped him take off into his dream. He was grounded in his chair. He did not even notice when Amy came round on her horse. She waved to him, and when he didn't respond, she decided that he was in his own world, and when he didn't wave on the second or the third round she noticed the despair on his up-turned face and she wished the ride would finish. He did not look at her until the merry-go-round slowed down, and then it was only with impatience to be off, and back home, and into his own room with the blinds drawn, and black all around him.

'What's the matter then, our Stan?'

He didn't answer. She started to wheel his chair, staring at the back of his head. Then she saw him clasp his hands round his shoulders, and grip them so tightly that his knuckles gleamed under the white skin. She couldn't understand it, but her heart turned over inside her.

'Want to go home, Stan?' she said. They were passing a shooting-gallery. Stan dropped his hands. 'Think I'll have a go with a rifle,' he said. His voice was gruff, almost unrecognisable.

'What's the matter, Stan?' she said again, wheeling him towards the stall.

'Nothing,' he practically shouted at her. 'Buy me a turn.'

For the first time in her life she was frightened of him. She wondered whether he was feeling ill. Now it was she who needed communication, and she regretted how often she had withheld it from him. She bought him three turns. At that moment she couldn't do enough for him. Anything in the world just so he wouldn't die or turn on her. She positioned his chair comfortable against the rail, and put the rifle in his hand.

A string of wooden ducks travelled along the eyeline, fixed on a rotating wheel, so that only six were visible at one time. Stan leaned his elbows on the rail and took aim. She noticed how steady his hands were, and how the strength gathered from his useless limbs bulged in his shoulders. She waited for him to fire, praying that he should not fail. Stan took his time, threatening each duck in turn. Then he steadied the rifle and fired. The leading duck fell first, then the following, and one by one he pulled twelve bull's eyes in succession until the rifle was empty. 'Another,' he shouted, not wanting to give a single resurrected duck a chance. His face was flushed with excitement, and Amy noticed how the vein in his temple throbbed. He grabbed the reloaded rifle, and Amy had her first and startling inkling of the violence that brewed inside him. He started shooting straight away and not a single duck survived his emptied gun. She thought that vein on his forehead would burst, and quickly she paid for yet another round.

The attendant would have been glad to get rid of Stan. He had already won two large teddy bears and he was due for a complete dinner service, that prize that had been gathering dust on the shelf from season to season, in and out of fashion. He closed his eyes and willed his poor old ducks to make a stand. But Stan felled them all until his gun was spent.

'That's enough now,' the man had to say, sadly taking the dinner service down from the shelf and wondering what new bait he could use till the end of the season. Stan exhaled with loud relief, as if during the whole duck slaughter he had held his breath. 'I'll hold it,' he said, taking the wrapped china on to his lap. She noticed how he sweated, and she touched his forehead. It was fire.

'We must go home, Stan,' she said.

He did not argue with her as she wheeled him to

the cab rank. She whispered the address to the driver. 'Quickly,' she pleaded. 'I think he's ill.' The driver lifted Stan into the cab, and folded his chair after him. All through the drive home Amy stared at her brother. She was now too terrified to ask how he was. About half way home Stan started to cough, not heavily, and with no phlegm, but with a fearful dry wheeze that echoed loudly through his breathing even when he was still. 'He mustn't die,' she willed to herself, clenching her fists by her side.

When they reached home the driver carried Stan to his bed like a bundle of baby in his arms, and Stan lay there quietly while Amy telephoned the doctor. He was calm in spite of his fever. He thought of the roundabout, and how all the backward doors had closed on him. As the lions and the horses had circled round his fixed and unstill centre, he had seen death approach and he had begun to surrender. His desperate firing at the shooting gallery had been perhaps a last and proud stand.

Dr Rhys arrived promptly. Amy stayed in the kitchen while he examined Stan. She did not go into the bedroom, both for Stan's sake and her own, and Dr Rhys would be in the kitchen with his verdict soon enough. She went into the hall and listened. She could hear Stan coughing, and the creak of the bed, and she stayed listening until she heard Dr Rhys moving towards the door, and then she went back into the kitchen.

'There now, Amy,' he said, jovial, seeing the worried look on her face. 'All right he is. Just a fever and his chest. But then you know his chest is bad, Amy. 'Tis his chest will carry him off. Not this time though. I've left some medicine. You should sit with him a little, Amy. He's low in spirit, I have the impression.'

'I'll go to him now,' she said, grateful to him, and seeing him to the door.

When he had gone she braced herself and knocked on Stan's door. She had never done that before. She had always barged into his room when and how she pleased. Stan coughed in reply and she went inside. She sat at his bedside, and felt his forehead. It was still very hot. 'It's all the excitement,' she said, keeping her voice calm. 'All that winning of yours at shooting. Soon as you're up and about, Stan, we'll have dinner off that set of yours. Invite Gwyneth. Show off a little bit.'

He managed to smile. 'There's good you are . . .' he started. But Amy put her hand on his and motioned him to save his strength. She held her hand there and wondered at it. She would normally have shuddered at the thought of any physical contact with her brother and she remembered ruffling his hair in the taxi, and now she was holding his hand. She thought it would repel her, or at least embarrass her a little, but it seemed natural to her and she was glad of it. She knew that something had happened to Stan at the roundabout, and that it was not all to do with his chest. She was unnerved too at his excitement at the shooting gallery, that had even less to do with his perfect aim. He turned his head towards her. 'I'm tired, Amy,' he said.

'Let's talk a little,' she pleaded, desperate to hold him from his surrender. She didn't believe Dr Rhys. She knew that Stan was dying but she had the naïve belief that if Stan could only keep his eyes open, Death would not catch him.

'Later,' he said. 'I want to sleep now.'

'Not for long though. I've made us a nice supper.'

She sat and watched him as he slept. In this same

bed, her Mam had died, and the room still held for her the horrors of that passing. She had died from the natural cause of anger, Amy-anger, mostly that she could never tame. Her rage had sprouted a cancer in her stomach, and her demise was slow and infinitely painful. Amy had almost loved her in those last few weeks when her Mam was too weak to shout at her. But the anger still raged in her Mam's eyes, that she should be reduced to dependency on one she had never been able to love. It made of her death an unintended apology, when, even in her dying heart, she wasn't sorry. Out of her sick eyes she still saw Amy's stubby nose, her over-neighbourly eyes and repellent chin, and it all added up to a grand let-down. After Stan, and his obvious frailty, she had so wanted a pretty little daughter, a doll to dress and tend, instead of this ungainly creature whom no amount of dressing could improve. As the end neared she asked for Stan more and more often. She never asked for Amy's Dad. He would come uninvited into the room, and in inno-cent and sad bewilderment he would sit by her bedside, holding her ungiving hand, and whispering, 'Stay with me, Gwen love.' Amy wondered why on earth he wished to prolong his punishment, why he couldn't envisage his splendid freedom once she had gone. It was only later on, when she and Stan were left alone, that she realised that habits, even those of suffering, are not easily broken.

'Where's Stan?' her Mam asked continually. 'Nobody looks after me,' she said, ignoring Amy and her Dad at her bedside. And Stan had to be called, and some-times even ordered to come, for he could not bear to witness the pain of his mother's death. Or so Amy had generously thought at the time. Later on, when it was all over, it was she and her Dad who had done the crying, and long and loud it was too. Stan had mourned not at all. Indeed he seemed almost relieved that she was no longer there, and Amy wondered whether, despite the hand-holding and the cuddling and the wooing of his childhood, he had really bitterly resented her and the rotten root she had planted inside him.

On her mercifully last day, Dr Rhys had left his verdict. She would not last the night. They sat with her, the three of them, and her Dad stared at his wife unbelieving. He no longer held her hand. With the last of her strength she had managed to draw it away. Amy could not look at her, but stared instead at Stan who was looking at his stamp collection. It was only his gaze that her Mam wanted, and he wouldn't give it to her. Amy hated him then.

'Give us your hand,' she heard her Mam say, and it was clear that she was not talking to her or to her Dad. Stan did not look up from his book, and her Dad, bursting from his poor wife's pain, grabbed Stan's gentle hand and placed it firmly on the counterpane before her. She took it with her feeble strength. Still he did not look at her. 'Who will look after you then, cariad, when I'm gone?' while Amy stood there, with her Dad, plain as bloody pikestaffs by the bed-side.

'I'll see to him, our Mam,' Amy said.

'But it's loving he needs,' her Mam managed to say, 'and there won't be much of that, though, will there?'

Those had been her last terrible words, and when Amy thought of them now, sitting by Stan's bed, she knew that her Mam had been right. There had been no loving from her to Stan. She had tried, but loving had dodged her. Now it seemed that it invaded her wholly, and she gripped Stan's hand.

'Give me another chance, Stan,' she whispered.

He stirred in his sleep and turned his head. She felt

his forehead. It was cool now, and she took it for his answer.

She left the room quietly to prepare supper. The evening newspaper lay on the hall floor, and without reading the headlines, even, she turned immediately to the Classified, greedy for the Personal Column as an addict for his fix. The pleas were more varied this time, with details of character and what attributes were sought. She went into the kitchen to study it. It's only a bit of fun, she kept telling herself, worried a little by the excitement the notices stirred in her. She felt guilty to be taking a little pleasure for herself while Stan was lying ill in the next room. She had faith that he would pull through this setback but, as Dr Rhys had said, she had to face the fact that her brother was a sickly man with few years left to him. Again she thought of the horror of a life without him, and she read the ads again to take her mind off such thoughts.

There were two or, at a push, three notices that she could reply to. She was 'presentable', 'home-loving', 'middle-aged', and above all, 'seeking companionship'. But the thought of being one out of dozens claiming these qualities, and more perhaps, exposed her to certain failure. The thought came to her of inserting her own request with the anonymity of a Box Number. She took the shopping-list pad from the mantlepiece and began chewing on the end of the pencil. 'It's only a bit of fun,' she said to herself again. 'Not going to send it, of course.' But already she was thinking of the possibility—for the very first time in her life—of choice, whatever the means. She began to giggle with excitement, anticipating collecting the post each morning and hiding the missives from Stan. For a moment she thought an advertisement for herself would prove an evil eye, and that Stan would die to make way for all her suitors. 'But it's only a bit of fun,' she said, chewing furiously on the end of the pencil.

She wondered how she should describe herself, whether she dared be honest with her opinion. She could lie by omission of course. There was no law against withholding the size and shape of one's nose in an advertisement, or any blemish that was only skin deep.

'Middle-aged Woman,' she wrote, then amended that to 'Lady'. Apart from giving a touch of class, the word sounded considerably thinner. 'Home-lover.' She wasn't too sure about the lover appendage. It was not an activity she could readily admit as her own, neither in a home nor in any other connection. It was a rude word anyway, she thought. Gwyneth would certainly have called it disgusting. So she wrote 'Home-maker', and was well pleased with it. She had to give some indication of her hobbies, her likes and dislikes, and although she had a string of the latter—at twopence a word, she could have bankrupted herself with all her loathings—there were few 'likes' that she could muster. So she settled for cooking and needlework and walks by the sea. As an afterthought she added, 'theatre', for from the other advertisements, that seemed to be the current marketable commodity. Only once in her life had she been to the theatre, and that was to a school-outing pantomime in Cardiff, but she had liked it well enough, so it was only half a lie she was admitting to. 'Wishing to meet gentleman,' she wrote on, and then, looking for a clue in the notices, she quoted, 'with similar needs.' She wasn't too happy with the word 'needs'. It sounded so exclusively sexual, and she noticed that she had bitten the end of the pencil through to the lead. But she left it at that, feeling very superior to Gwyneth.

She read it over and it pleased her. 'It's only a bit of fun,' she said, though she was not giggling any more. She knew she had to enclose a letter to the paper, asking for a Box Number and giving her name and address. The latter was straightforward enough, for to lie about it would cause her great inconvenience with collection. But she balked at giving her real name. Even though she knew few people in Cardiff, it was not impossible that one of them knew somebody who worked in the Classified Department of the *Welsh Echo*. Suddenly she had a great sense of self-importance that the eye of the world turned on the comings and goings of Amy Evans of Porthcawl. No, it wouldn't do. She'd give herself a new persona. At this point, she bit the end of the pencil clean off, and she started nibbling again on the pristine wood. She thought of what name she could re-baptise herself with. As a child, she'd always wanted to be called Blodwen. Blodwens always played harps, and in her child's eye they were angels. Yes, Blodwen it would be, and Pugh, as the end of the handle, for that name belonged to the posh shop on the pier where you could buy dresses made in Paris, and trousers too, whatever Gwyneth might think. So Blodwen Pugh it was, and she signed it with a flourish. Automatically she enclosed it in brackets. Even in her alibi she could only see herself in inferior parenthesis.

As she addressed the envelope, she still thought it was a bit of fun. There was the postal order and the posting to be done before it could be called serious. And the post offices were closed now, and the last post gone. Tomorrow in the morning she would think it had been a good joke, but not quite funny enough, she thought, to share with Gwyneth.

She went back into Stan's room. He was still sleeping. His breathing was easy now, and without wheeze.

Perhaps he would sleep through the night, she thought, and she would leave her bedroom door open if he called. As she ate her supper alone, she decided to go into Pugh's the following day and, when no one was looking, she would try on a pair of French trousers.

*　　*　　*

He was better in the morning and had made tea before Amy got up, and when she came into the kitchen he was already reading the morning paper. He was cheerful, and Amy's fears dissolved. When she'd woken, she'd remembered about the advertisement and she had seen it once more as a bit of fun, until Stan, marking off a mail-order offer of a stamp catalogue, asked her to drop into the post office for a registered envelope. It seemed as if he were willing her to post the letter. As long as she could think about it as Stan's decision, she personally felt less involved, and as she bought the postal order along with Stan's envelope, it was as if she were buying both for Stan. She posted her letter in the box 'Stan's bit of fun,' she said to herself, and as she turned away, she began to count the days until she could confidently expect a stream of replies. This being a Saturday, she couldn't expect her little plea to appear until Tuesday. By Thursday a goodly number of wooers would be pressing their suit to her Box Number, and by Friday morning the offers would begin to pour in.

On her way home, she made a detour to Pugh's on the pier. Her courage of the night before had left her. She wouldn't try on a pair of trousers. She would just look at them in the window. But even to stop at Pugh's window required an act of courage. It was a pavement area for well-dressed ladies who had the taste and the money to seriously consider using both. She hesitated before stopping, for a pair of feather-hatted ladies were politely glued to the pane. When they passed on, she took their scented place, and once having stopped she gathered confidence. The trousers from Paris draped round three skinny dummies and were in different colours. She didn't know why they attracted her so and when she saw the reflection of her own figure between the glass and the models she was sadly assured that they were not for her. But it nagged at her, that they would make her slim, daring even, and it was time anyway to change the non-style she had worn all her life.

She found herself inside the shop and at the trouser counter. An assistant approached before she could lose her courage.

'It's for my sister,' she said, wavering, but suddenly inspired. 'A pair of those trousers from Paris in the window.'

'What size, Madam?'

'Well,' Amy giggled, 'we're both the same. You see, she doesn't live in Porthcawl. In Cardiff she lives. But she swears you don't get the like in Cardiff. Fancy, a big city with no French clothes.' She would have been happy to continue discussion of the sartorial inadequacies of the metropolis, to commiserate with a city that was not blessed with an establishment like Pugh's, in order to make the girl take more kindly to her ugliness, but the assistant was already sizing her up in a professional manner.

'Now I don't think we have your size, Madam,' she said. 'If we have, then it's only black. But black in any case is best for a big woman.' Amy became timid again and agreed with her heartily. She could have hugged the girl if only for her lack of sneer.

The girl went over to the rail and picked out the

largest she could find. 'This way,' she said, as if taking Amy's decision to try them on. She led her to a cubicle, hung the trousers on a hanger, and hovered. 'I'll manage,' Amy said, terrified, not wanting this young and skinny girl to view her ageing body, and the girl, understanding, withdrew.

'I'll be at the counter,' she said, 'if you want me.'

Amy drew the curtain firmly and turned her back to the mirror. It was a long time since she had actually looked at her own body. Such courage as she had, had already been overspent on entering the shop and ordering. It would take a monumental act of heroism to face a mirror unclothed. So she undressed hurriedly in a corner, hiding her nakedness even from itself. She started to put on the trousers. The feel of new clothes was exciting. She drew them on carefully, getting each foot into each leg, before she dared draw them up on her thighs. She pulled slowly and with growing confidence as she noticed that the material could stretch. Miraculously, they covered her thighs without complaint, and then she stopped, praying for a miracle. Shutting her eyes tight she prepared for the final haul, and with a little sweating she made it. Even the zip closed without too much resistance, though it forced her midriff over her stomach like a drooping curtain. She was nervous to turn around and look at herself, so she felt herself first, and she found it comfortable and good. Her eyes still closed, she turned to face the mirror. One, two, three, she counted to herself before she opened them, and even then, she avoided her face, looking strictly into the lower half of the glass. She was surprised. She did indeed look a great deal thinner, and she was overcome by such joy that she forgot about her face and saw it smiling back at her in the mirror. 'It's only a bit of fun,' she said to it, and quickly she took the trousers off, dressed, and paid for them at the counter. She would have to hide the bag from Stan. He wouldn't understand it at all. Of course, she had no intention of wearing them, ever it seemed, except perhaps when she came to know her chosen suitor very well, perhaps on her honeymoon if they went to Paris, and then she would look absolutely right. She was so excited with her purchase, that the girl had to run after her with her change.

'You'll be losing your head,' the girl laughed, handing her the money.

Amy took the short cut over the sand dunes to her house. It was years since she had passed this way. It was too precarious a surface for Stan's chair, and when alone she had never been in haste to get home. But now she was beginning to like home a little, and Stan in it too, and its letterbox that over the next week would receive her heavy choice-riddled future. She didn't want to leave it any more, except to be carried over the threshold to a new one. As she imagined it, Stan would wheel his chair in after them. It would be like what the rude French called a Menage a Troice. She wasn't quite sure what it meant. She would ask Gwyneth. Like everything else, Gwyneth would know that too. She wondered at herself and this sudden onset of joy inside her. It was only hope, that's all it was, that made the difference, the possibility of some change in her monotonous life. She did not think for one moment that her hopes would come to nothing. Advertising paid, that's what everybody said. How they would celebrate, she thought, with Gwyneth eating her heart out and choking on the champagne. 'Met him on a bus, I did, Gwyneth, on the way to Porth to get Stan a new pullover. Got to talking. Ever so polite he was, offering to carry my parcel. A real gent. Not many of them around, Gwyneth, only one in fact. You'll have to go without, I'm afraid. But you can still bring the bread round in the morning, if it's not too far like, like Paris abroad, or London perhaps. Now you go a bit easier on that champagne, Gwyneth, or you'll end up like our Dad.'

She stopped walking. She rarely thought of her Dad now. Not since he had passed over, and Stan taking up most of her heart. She had loved her Dad, and he, her, she knew, so there was no remorse when remembering him. Just sadness at the way he had to go.

When her Mam had died in horrible pain, with eyes and syllables only for Stan, he had begun to talk to his late wife more than he had ever done in her lifetime. In the evenings, Amy could hear him in his room talking to her about the children when they were young, his mayoral days, and sometimes dwelling on specifics, like picnics they had taken together or masonic dinners. It kept him going for a while until he feared for his mind. So he turned to God, a devotion that would at least make his lunacy acceptable. The Salvation Army was glad to welcome him as a member, and he was happy as a boy with his new uniform. He went a bit overboard with the God business. Now in his room he talked to Jesus, in non-stop euphoric adulation. Amy was happy to let it be, and wouldn't have given it another thought had she not made a trifle and noticed that the sherry bottle was empty. Her Dad was out at the time, beating his drum to Jesus on the pier. He couldn't blow and he couldn't sing, so they'd given him a small side drum so that he shouldn't feel out of things. When she'd last made a trifle the bottle had been almost full, and it occurred to her that its emptiness now probably accounted for her Dad's constant peppermint breath. 'Disgusting,' she said, automatically, and then, 'Poor Dad.' She went to his room and opened his cupboard. She was not surprised to see the bottles there and she left them, because she did not want it known that she knew, because she simply could not deal with that knowledge. She didn't tell Stan either, and she lived with it alone and with terrible pity.

As the weeks passed, his love-songs to Jesus grew louder and more passionate, and the peppermint breath was staggering. He was hitting God and the bottle with equal exuberance, and Amy feared that soon it would be in the open and she could ignore it no longer. One day he came home from an Army meeting and he hit it hard. She heard him stumbling about in his room. She listened outside the door. There was no talk to Jesus this time, just the loud painful retch of his vomiting. She went inside.

'Stomach trouble,' he said helplessly, holding an empty sherry bottle and staring at the vomit spreading over his tunic.

'Something I ate,' he said.

'I'll tidy you up a bit,' Amy said, letting it pass, and thereafter he took off his uniform as soon as he came into the house, and in his underpants he sang aloud to Jesus.

Amy hid her cooking sherry now, but she still made a trifle on a Sunday as she had done since her Mam had died. Outwardly she wanted no change. But she knew that her Dad was getting worse. Stan knew about it now. Her Dad's holy ravings were so loud that the neighbours probably knew about it too. But more worrying than the volume of his devotions was their changing style. Before, her Dad had been satisfied with the Scriptures, ranting them by rote and with fervour. But now he was adapting them to his own personal needs, and his psalms were laced with ardent obscenities. It was as if he were verbalising a lifetime of frustration, a thousand and one nights of love foregone. Now he indemnified himself for his body's loss with much filth and devious imaginings, yet with just enough of the Authorised Version to give himself cover. Amy listened outside his door. 'Disgusting,' she would say to herself, and then stop and eavesdrop, restraining her enjoyment. Stan said nothing, though it was impossible not to hear his Dad's ravings or not to notice his reeling gait and minted breath. Stan closed into himself and smiled, much as he had done when his Mam stretched out to him her dying hand. His attitude worried Amy. He seemed unwilling to be moved by anything. 'Our Dad's a drunk,' she shouted at him one day, and again the saintly smile and silence. So she coped with her Dad alone, understanding him, pitying him, keeping his slippery secret. Sometimes she hoped her Dad would die before it was out and booted round the town. He still kept his sense of ex-mayoral reputation. The death of his wife could have driven him to God. Or even to drink. Either would have been acceptable. But to be driven to both, each feeding on the other with parasitic appetite, was a proposition that Porthcawl simply would not stomach. And she and Stan would be left with a sour hangover of rumour and scandal which no amount of denial would gainsay.

He began to keep more and more to his room, and only went out for Army parades and drum thumping. Amy kept his uniform pressed and clean, and it hung over his drums in the hall closet. It was a blessing, she supposed, that he did not use his drum to accompany his ravings. It is possible the thought had occurred to him, but was promptly dismissed since he wanted nothing to soft-pedal the filth of his adoration.

His secret stayed indoors, muted by the dividing

walls for over a year, and would have died with him had it not been for the Easter Parade.

'I'll go up now, love, and change,' he said after breakfast, though it was a good few hours before the assembly. She heard him ranting in his room and dreaded his appearance in what could only be a firing line. She took him his uniform at the last moment, passing it through the door. And she waited.

He looked smart enough, though his gait was unsteady. She hooked the drum over his shoulder and put the sticks in his hand. As he staggered down the path to the street, bent under the weight of his banger, he looked like an aged drummer-boy going to war, and when he turned to wave goodbye she felt with a stab of pain, suddenly orphaned. She followed him at a distance. It was only a few hundred yards to the assembly ground where they were to have a musical warm-up before proceeding by charabanc to the pier. She stood on the perimeter of the ground, along with a crowd of locals and relatives who had come to give them a send-off. The band arranged itself in a holy semi-circle, about twelve of them. Amy noticed that they gave her Dad the collecting box, a heavy black leaden container, and she saw him falter under its empty weight. No doubt the Army felt that with the small crowd present they could profit a little even if only rehearsing. No one but herself seemed to notice her Dad's tremblings, or possibly they attributed them to the cold or approaching old age. She saw one of the trumpeters pat him affectionately on the back, near enough, she swore, to have had a sniff of his minted breath. The gulls shrieked overhead, and settled on the rocks to listen to the band, which struck up, ambitiously enough, with 'Jerusalem'. Amy did not hear them. She was staring straight at her Dad, watching his lips move, but certainly not with the words of the hymn. He was tapping his foot to the beat of the drum and she saw how his shiny black boot gleamed in the cold spring sun. Then the boot stopped, as did his beating, while his mouth opened wider with his praises, and his face was suffused with an almost liquid joy. She dreaded the end of the hymn. But when it came, his mouth shut too, and he lurched over to the crowd for the collection. As he came towards them, he saw Amy. Amy had often wondered later on whether it had been the sight of her that had prompted his fatal giveaway. Whatever the reason, he stopped when he saw her. 'Duw mun,' he shouted across the parade ground. 'What d'you know then? Our Amy cariad, come to be saved. Come, come, come to share a fuck with Jesus,' a phrase he repeated loudly to the tune of 'Once in Royal David's City', for in his state it was always Christmas. His filth sang out over the parade ground in a thin and grating paean, like a tired crowing of a cock after his congress. The silence around was piercing. Even the gulls ceased their cry. When he'd made his praises clear, her Dad sat down, not from fatigue, but that he was not able to stand on his feet any longer. His drum was between his knees, and he was unable to stop the collecting box falling through its skin. His poor head followed into the topless drum. And inside it he was sick. Nice and tidy.

Amy moved towards him. What surprised her was the stream of blood flowing through the drum. She lifted his head, and found its source. A vessel had burst in his temple where he had struck it on the corner of the iron box. His eyes were glazed and a spittle of vomit drooped on his chin. Suddenly the gulls started to cry, and take off from their perches, and hover like vultures over the sea. She was glad when the ambulance came and took him away, away from the incredulous stare of the crowd, the gathering rumour that by nightfall would spread around the town, passing and magnifying from mouth to mouth, to salivate in unison at his funeral.

Amy took it bad. Stan nodded his curly head, and hid a saintly smile, and she wondered whether all his life, from his iron-clad to wheel-chair days, he had colonised and hated them all for creating and making such a puppet of him. At their Dad's funeral he had positively turned his head away from the open grave. Amy knew he was hiding a smile of benign satisfaction, and she wondered whether he had it in mind to outlive her too.

*　　*　　*

With her pair of French trousers from Paris, France, Amy Evans started her bottom drawer. As soon as the expected letters came and she had made her choice, she would buy linen and embroidery thread. She giggled uncontrollably at the thought of buying new nightwear, and of stitching her initial on the bodice, naughtily entwined with his. Of course, she realised she would have to come clean about the Blodwen Pugh alibi, but by then Amy Evans, in the ears of her intended, would be a song of love, and in any case, through marriage, she would shortly lose half of it.

Over the next few days, she was so bound up in her fantasies that she was startled when Stan began to talk about their plans for Christmas as if nothing on earth was going to interrupt them. The time was still expectant. It would be another three days at least before she could reasonably expect the first of her replies.

The following day, when the advertisement

appeared, she hid the evening paper from Stan until she could check on it herself. She tore it open to the Classified to read her self advertisement with hot blushes. Again she feared that someone in Porthcawl would guess it might be she, but reading it over and over again she could confidently find nothing that would identify her. So she gave it to Stan and watched him closely as he turned the pages, and she sighed with relief as he passed over the Classified. She was very restless and felt the need to occupy herself continually. She would spring clean the house. Tomorrow was Gwyneth's day for taking Stan. Every Thursday she would wheel him home with her after breakfast, and during the morning she let him help her in the shop. It was early closing day, and sometimes in the afternoon she would take him to the pier to listen to the band.

As soon as they were gone Amy decided to make a start on Stan's room, since she was rarely able to have it to herself for any length of time to clean thoroughly. She saw them off down the path already regretting that in future Gwyneth would come less often. She resolved that her future husband would have to befriend Gwyneth too. She wasn't too bad, and she did, after all, know everything.

She started on Stan's bed. It was a long time since she had turned the mattress. Even her annual spring-cleaning hadn't called for that. But this time it was going to be thorough. No intended of hers, she swore, was going to think her a common slut. She dragged the mattress off with all that determination and saw the plain wrapped envelopes underneath. She thought it was a strange place to keep his stamp catalogues, that collection for which every week she bought him a registered envelope. She gathered them into a pile to put them on his shelf. As she carried them across the room, some of their contents fell on to the floor. She noticed that what the plain envelopes contained were light-years away from healthy catalogues. She squatted on the floor to make a closer examination, and after a preliminary perusal she got up and locked Stan's door, for though she hardly expected anybody she dared not risk intrusion. Then she made herself comfortable on a cushion on the floor, and started a thorough investigation.

'Disgusting', she said, at every photograph, and having given them her normal judgement she settled into looking at them in detail. There were about two hundred in all, ten in each of the twenty envelopes. They were pictures of the sort of things even Gwyneth wouldn't have known anything about. Men and women together in the most outrageous positions, some with bodies unnaturally grotesque. She knew what they were doing of course, she had had personal experience of that, so she could vouch for the fact that it certainly was going on in the world, but never had she imagined such positioning. In some pictures a dog was involved in the coupling, and in others, two women and one man. There were men together, and women too. Gwyneth could never have heard of all that. She felt herself blushing, and she again murmured, 'disgusting', now with more fervour, to offset the enjoyment of her viewing. She laid the cards out on the floor for an accumulated impression, and her excitement was almost unbearable. Suddenly she realised that these pictures belonged to Stan, and that her interest lay less in the pictures themselves than in what they revealed of her brother. Disgusting. But something about it pleased her. If she could find such excitement in the pictures, so could Stan, and what a relief it must be to his chair-bound life to fly occasionally into a throbbing if substitute Eden. Perhaps the memory of these pictures was what was hidden in his continual smile, the saintliness of which was as much cover for his voyeurism as the Bible had been for her Dad's sweet sherry. She put them back carefully into their envelopes and replaced them where she had found them. She wished Stan joy of them. Now that she expected a suitor by any post after tomorrow, she would be more generous in her tolerance of human failings. A man with the constant love of a woman would not need such pictures for company. Stan was entitled, most deservedly. She dragged the mattress back over the packets, still trembling with excitement. Only another two days, she thought, and her love would come, not on a white charger perhaps, but through a box number and a letterbox, but that need not make it less true.

She hurried with the cleaning now. She wanted to positively wait out the days with nothing to interfere with the waiting. In her recent excited anticipations she had learned that time passed quickly, and when Stan came back in the evening it seemed only a few minutes ago that she had discovered the secret of his smile. She tried to pretend that nothing had happened, but now, at supper, she found herself embarrassed to be with him, seeing him gloating over those obscenities in his room at night, and probably half the day as well, when he was supposed to be sorting out his stamps. She found herself slightly angry with him that he had pulled such a fast one on her, and she going out all those years of weeks to buy him his registered envelope. But he was entitled to his secrets after all. There was little of his life that he could for ever keep private. At times, when he was very ill, she had to feed him, dress and bathe him. She had witnessed his occasional

incontinence, his ugly wheezings, and his naked mal-
formed body. She should be able to leave his mind,
however sordid, to himself. She wished now she had
never found the postcards and she smiled across the
table at him in the hope of forgiving herself. But now
his returning smile reflected those dreadful couplings
underneath his mattress, and she knew that something
between them had irrevocably changed, and that only
she was aware of it. She wished again that she had
never found them. When he said he'd have an early
night she knew exactly why, and she tried to wish him
joy of them.

While she was washing up she tried not to think of
what he was doing, for even that excited her, and such
excitement was disgusting. She fought it down, knowing inside herself that she was jealous of him, that in
spite of his cabinned life he had ammunition enough
for flights of fancy. So she would count the hours till
the letterbox rattled, so that in time she and Stan would
be evens.

The following day was hard to swallow. The last
day before commitment. Stan was well and smiling
and she was cross with him. He had dirtied his room
again, and though she refrained from telling him of
her minor spring clean she was none the less angry
with him for his inconsideration. 'What will my husband say?' was the constant thought at the back of her
head, and it worried her that her notion of reality had
become so unreliable. And so she was angrier with
Stan, and the more he smiled at her and apologised
the more her fury rose. By supper time, she was positively shouting at him, bemoaning the way he had
ruined her life. It was cruel, she knew, so cruel, but
with her Waterloo arriving in the morning, and the
possibility of it ending in a rousing defeat—for even

in her wildest daydreams the fear of total failure had never entirely left her—she shivered with anxiety for her lonely Stan-less future.

She went to bed early, too, that night, following soon after Stan. But she couldn't sleep. Now there were only hours to count before the postman came, and she feared for all the hopes she had pinned on his delivery. In the middle of the night she went downstairs to make herself tea. She heard Stan stirring and she tried not to think of what he was doing. So she called out to him, 'Stan, would you like a cup of tea?'

He answered quickly and happily. He was wide awake, and no doubt at his viewing. She heard a quick rustling of paper as she went into the kitchen. Four more hours to go, she reckoned, then all her waiting would be over and only joy would come.

She took in Stan's tea, being careful to knock first on the door. He was smiling of course, and full of gratitude and concern at her inability to sleep. He wanted to talk about plans for Christmas, but she pleaded a headache, begging him to keep them till the morning. Perhaps then she might have news for him, or no news at all, and her heart gulped at the thought that this Christmas would be the same as the last, and the next, and all the monotonous ones to come.

She trudged back to her bed, and listened as the chapel bell tolled the hour. At seven o'clock fatigue overcame her, and though she tried to fight it, since delivery was so close, she fell asleep, not to wake again until well after the post had arrived. Her first thought on waking was the letterbox, and then Stan's breakfast, and why Gwyneth was so late. She rushed down to the kitchen where Gwyneth was cutting the bread, and Stan eating it with home-made jam, and the post, or lack of it, on the kitchen table. The gas-bill, loud and clear through its window envelope, and nothing more.

'Is that all,' she said, picking it up.

'What were you expecting then. A billet-doux?'

Stan joined in Gwyneth's laughter. Then he saw Amy's drawn face and he motioned Gwyneth to be quiet.

'I've got such a headache,' Amy said covering up and wanting to get back to her bed to weep out her dire disappointment. But a cup of tea cheered her a little, and when Gwyneth offered to take Stan for the day she was relieved. She could then be depressed if she had to, without having Stan around with his saintly concern. In any case, today was only the first possibility. There were at least three more days in which she could justifiably nurture her hopes.

But the following day the postbox was empty. And the day after. Yet she refused to give up hope. A man didn't reply in haste to such an advertisement. He had to take his time to describe himself, to present himself in such a light as would be acceptable. And he would be a busy man too, at work all day, with only the evenings to relax in. Moreover he was intelligent, so he would give his answer much thought. Indeed, she deduced, it was as well the replies had not arrived post haste. Such speed would have betrayed a lack of seriousness. She was happily prepared to wait until the morning.

Stan was in a cheerful mood when Gwyneth delivered him that evening. He'd spent most of the time with Gwyneth's brother, Huw, who'd come up from Bridgend for the day. They had been close friends through school, but then the war came and they had lost touch with each other, as had most of Stan's friends. Perhaps they envied him a little for his exemption. A group of them had been shipped overseas with the Welsh regiment. Four of them were killed in the first few months of the war, and many more were wounded. Huw himself had lost an arm, but he'd managed to get a job as a counter-hand in a grocer's shop in Bridgend. Later he'd married the owner's daughter and now the shop was his. He owned the shop more than he did his wife, who was known even as far off as Porthcawl as having an eye for a bit of spare. Lately he'd been coming more and more often to Porthcawl to spend the day with Gwyneth. He had an artificial arm now with cumbersome claw fingers. He had acquired it years after his injury, during which time he had happily adapted himself to a one-armed existence. He found the limb something of a handicap, and quite often he just wouldn't put it on, but Gwyneth insisted that he wear it on his Porthcawl visits for fear of what the neighbours might say. But she was in the shop most of the afternoon, so in the back kitchen Huw took it off and laid it on the table while he and Stan played draughts.

Stan had found the arm unnerving, especially the nerveless claw section of the hand. He was better off than Huw, he thought. At least his limbs, such as they were, were flesh and a little blood, almost useless, but alive and a natural part of him. He understood why Huw didn't want to wear it. It called attention to the death in him, to his part-by-part dissolution, and when Gwyneth came unexpectedly into the kitchen and Huw picked up his wooden arm it was the meek and gentle Stan who tore it from him. 'Why don't you throw it away, boyo?' he said, daring Gwyneth to protest. ' 'Sno good to you. You manage better without.'

Gwyneth's anger burst. She was not going to be over-ruled in her own kitchen. 'I suppose *you'd* like him in the chair beside you,' she spat at him.

'Oh, Gwyneth,' Huw said, 'there's a terrible thing to say about our Stan.' And Gwyneth was sorry and said so immediately, and told Huw not to bother since no one was likely to come into the kitchen. Stan sensed a small victory on Huw's behalf, which was why he was so cheerful when he came home.

Amy tried to match his mood. Whatever would be in the post for her in the morning had clearly been posted by now, so that her fate, such as it might be, was already sealed. She would manage to get through the rest of the day, but what worried her most was how she could sustain herself after tomorrow, should no delivery come. Had she any right at all to hope any longer, for a further day at most? She went about building her preventive defences. It was possible that after a long day's work her suitors would spend the evening writing to her, and then it would be too late to catch the evening post. Yes, she could fairly give herself one more day after the next.

And it was just as well. For the morning post brought no more than the annual circular from the Salvation Army announcing their Christmas arrangements. She found the day particularly hard to swallow, for she knew that she only had one more chance. Then she would have to give up hope for ever, and resign herself to a future that was totally alone. There was always Gwyneth of course, but she was becoming more crotchety and irritable. The smaller the range of Gwyneth's life-experience, the larger her knowledge. More and more often, she knew everything. She had long ago ceased to pronounce on the subject of sex. No doubt she felt she had schooled Amy well enough in that quarter, and if it inadvertently slipped into the conversation, she felt it enough to dismiss it as disgusting. Now it was politics about which she knew everything.

All communists were evil. Black people were barbarians, no matter how much you tried to help them. She knew for a fact that what with all these fertility pills and messing around with your body, lots of two-headed babies were being born. 'Course, they try to hide it, Amy, but two I heard of in Porth only the other day. Two in a small place like Porth. Multiply that if you can. Duw, I don't know what it's coming to. The government should do something,' she said in despair. Everything was going to pieces, the price of butter, no one in chapel what d'you expect, and all those fat Jew landlords. She had a list of grievances, and when she ran out she started again, and with her last ounce of breath she would sum it all up. Disgusting.

Amy would listen and be bored. Inside her she knew that Gwyneth talked a lot of rubbish, but she was too timid to protest, and Gwyneth in any case would brook no argument. She was the only friend Amy had, and when her mouth was shut she was a good friend indeed. She helped Amy often enough with Stan. Gwyneth would miss him almost as much as she. But Amy turned off such thoughts. She had one more chance before she must entertain them. She was irritable with Stan all day and would have left him alone had he not started to wheeze with the onset of a new attack. Her irritation at having to look after him in his ill spells was equal to the fear that this one would be his last. She hated her anger with him. She began to regret having written to the paper at all. It had changed her, all that terrible hoodwinking hope. She took him his medicine and had to spoon it into his mouth, his hands were trembling so. Usually when he was taken ill she felt very tender towards him, but now she even shouted at him for dribbling the brown staining medicine on to his pyjamas. His spluttering apology made it worse, and she was angry enough to kill him on the spot. She had to leave his room quickly for fear of her own violence.

She sat in the kitchen and hoped sincerely and heartily that a letter would never come. That an end would be assured to all her sickly hopes, and that she would learn to like herself a little more and to live with herself alone. She opened the evening paper, turning automatically to the Classified. So many lonely love-seeking people. What chance did she stand amongst them all, with her stubby nose, her close-set eyes, her jutting chin with no matter how golden a heart and soul. A ripple of self pity lapped at her. She was not normally given to such feelings and she knew them as a danger signal. She would pull herself together, she decided. Tomorrow, after the post had been and gone, she would find other reasons for living.

She made sure that Stan was sleeping, then she went to bed herself, leaving her door ajar. She wanted desperately to sleep, but hope kept her restless still. The night passed for her in fitful snatches of dozing, and when she rose in the morning she both hoped and feared that the letterbox would be empty. Which it was.

She determined to give the matter no more thought. She went straight to Stan's room and found that he was still sleeping. She noticed that he had tossed the bedclothes off during the night, as if he'd been in fever, but now, although his breathing was full of wheeze, his forehead was cool. She went into the kitchen to make tea. 'I must give up hope,' she said, and she said it out loud and clear, as if she needed something, even the four walls, to bear witness to her decision. She had made a mistake in allowing her hopes to be raised. But no one would ever find out, and she would get over it.

Even the trousers from Paris, France, would remain a secret. She tried to find something ridiculous in the whole non-event. She attempted a smile, but vainly, for she had to acknowledge that hope still gnawed like a rat inside her.

She had to feed Stan, and again the mess he made would infuriate her. He hadn't woken up before eleven o'clock, and she'd had to keep his porridge going for hours. As she was spooning it down him, she heard the rattle of the letterbox. She practically dropped the spoon on to the blankets. 'There's the second post,' Stan said needlessly.

She willed herself to stay there until the porridge was finished. She was glowing again. Excitement flushed her with honeymoon thoughts, sweet together-nights, embroidered trousseau. When Stan had finished she hesitated before leaving. She couldn't face disappointment again, having resolved only a few moments before to think no more of her folly.

'What you waiting for then?' Stan said.

'Nothing,' she faltered. 'I'll be back with your tea.'

She carried the tray out and saw the letter in the box. She went first into the kitchen to deposit the tray, and then slowly into the hall to know what was to become of her. One letter. One single reply. That was enough, she thought, even glad that there would be no need for choice.

It came from the newspaper office and was addressed to Blodwen Pugh. She had almost forgotten her alias, and she marvelled at how important the name looked in printed letters. Inside the envelope was another, addressed to her box number. She took it into the kitchen. She noticed how her hand trembled as she opened the letter, and she shut her eyes, laying it flat on the table. She took a deep breath, the very first, she assured herself, of her infinitely exciting rebirth.

Before opening her eyes, she decided to concentrate first on the address, and to wring out of it a mine of information as to the character and class of her so beautiful suitor. She opened her eyes as slowly as she was able to prolong the almost unbearable excitement. Then she read the address.

A scream of pain uncoiled slowly inside her, as she spelled out the location of her own and terrible home. The house where she had been born, where her stubby nose had grown stubbier, where her Mam grew a cancer of Amy-anger, where her Dad, sweet-sherried, had coupled Jesus to his death. She heard her own tortured cry as it rose from her bowel, as she checked, quite needlessly now, on the signature. Stan Evans. Proud and clear.

'Oh,' she screamed, 'I'll fucking well break every bone in your fucking body. I'll smash your fucking pretty face in. I'll . . .'

His wheezing rattled suddenly through the corridor and she ran to him. Her anger dissolved in the space of reaching him, first into fear as she sat him up to ease his coughing, and then into love that willed him for God's sake not to leave her. She gave him some medicine. Now when he spilled it she almost blessed him. She would forgive him everything if only he would go on living.

'There's good you are to me, Amy,' he managed to say between coughs, and his gratitude did not irk her. Instead she saw him sitting at his desk a few days before, painfully spelling out to some misty newspaper stranger the sad alphabet of his loneliness. He must have posted the letter when Gwyneth had taken him

out. He would have told her it was for a stamp catalogue, that fantasy of his that covered everything.

'Why are you smiling then, our Amy?' he said.

'Nothing,' she said.

He seemed better now, but tired, needing to sleep
after the coughing fit that had racked him. She was
anxious now to leave the room, to go back to the kitchen to read his letter. She closed his door quietly, and
the kitchen door too, for her reading would require
the utmost privacy, as much for Stan as for herself. The
letter lay on the table, and she flattened out the four
meticulous folds.

'Dear Miss Advertiser,' she read, and she wondered
when she saw the handwriting why she had not recognised it immediately from the envelope. The possibility
of a reply from Stan had been so remote, and her over-
excitement had suspended her normal perception. Now
it seemed to her right and proper that the only reply
she had received to her plea for companionship and
care should have been from her brother.

'I saw your advertisement in the *Echo* last week,' she
read, 'and I am writing in reply. Sorry it's late, but it's
a bit difficult, I'm sure you will agree, to write this
kind of letter. In any case, I kept thinking that you
would get hundreds of replies and I didn't see much
point in adding to the number, so every day I put off
writing. But now I've decided to have a go, and I hope
you will view my application with favour.'

The phrase made her smile. It recalled all those
letters of job application that Stan had written at their
Dad's dictation, when he'd left school. Whether it was
a job as letter-sorter at the post office, munitions packer,
filing clerk, each letter started off with a list of his
handicaps, implying that he was no bargain to anybody, and ended with the plea to view his application

with favour. This time he had not listed his drawbacks. Perhaps they were to come later. As indeed they began, in the next sentence.

'I have to tell you straight away that I am a cripple.' She started at this word. Ever since she could remember, the word had been a taboo in the house. A sickly child, or a sickly boy was the threshold of description. 'Cripple' was a word that cruel schoolchildren used, or charitable do-gooders, accompanying it with a pat on the head. Stan would weep whenever he heard it. Now he was using it himself, with pride even, and as she read the letter, with such repetition, that it almost seemed to give him pleasure. 'I am confined to a wheelchair,' he wrote, 'as a result of a childhood attack of rickets. I have not been able to walk for many years, but I have a great strength in my arms and my torso.'

She trembled at the word. It seemed to her that in a letter to an anonymous box number it was oddly intimate, and with growing excitement she read on. 'I don't have much opportunity to use it of course, because I have very few friends.'

She wondered what sort of friendship her brother was offering. She had an uneasy feeling that his letter had been clearly influenced by his study of sub-mattress culture. 'I do not live alone, because I am not able to look after myself. At least, that's what everybody says, but I think that I would do it very well, and who knows, one day, I may have to.'

Suddenly she saw him attending her own funeral, throwing a shovelful of earth on to the grave, but looking elsewhere with his saintly smile. She was surprised at how little she minded. She was beginning to regard him as a stranger. 'I live with my sister,' she read on. 'Her name is Amy, and although she hates it I think it is one of the prettiest names on earth. Perhaps I think that because she is so beautiful.'

Amy put the letter down, her head spinning. Till that sentence, there had been no doubt about the truth of his words. Or at least his kind of truth. It was not like Stan to play games. There was no triviality about him. Did he honestly believe she was beautiful? She ran her hands over her stubby face, and her fingers throbbed with the ugliness her Mam had insisted on. She got up and looked in the mirror over the mantle-piece. One would be hard pressed, she had to admit, to find that face beautiful, and she went back to the letter to see if Stan had provided any proof.

'She has beautiful hair, the colour of sand, which she ties back in a bun. I've often wished she would let it loose, so that she wouldn't look like my nurse all the time.'

Again she went to the mirror and quickly unpinned her hair. Stan was right. It softened her. But she couldn't let it loose. There must be no grounds for even the remotest suspicion. Over the next few weeks, she would let it happen by accident, and hope for his approval. She went back to the letter.

'Amy looks after me like an angel. Nothing is too much for her. Sometimes I worry that she has sacri-ficed her life to me, for she never got married, and I think now that it is too late. I think that if ever I could make a real friend of somebody, it would be somebody like Amy. I wish I knew your name, Miss Advertiser. I feel silly writing like this into the blue. I hope you will reply to me. You see from my address I live near the sea. Our house overlooks Rest Bay in Porthcawl, and I know every inch of sand along it. Because although I am a cripple, there was a time when I was a child that I could run over the sands and dunes, or climb the rocks jutting over the sea. I would love to tell you all about my childhood adventures. Oh I am so praying that you will reply to me.'

Yes. That's what he wanted, Amy thought. All those memories that she denied him. This was his under-standing of companionship, a mutual sharing of history. She turned to the last paragraph.

'Although I am a cripple, it is only in my limbs,' he went on. 'I can offer you the wholeness of my heart and spirit, and I mean that most sincerely. I am, Yours truly, Stan Evans. P.S. Please reply. If you do, would you send me a snap?'

Amy had the strange feeling that she had opened someone else's letter, hoping that whoever was the recipient would answer immediately to his plea. At the same moment she knew that it was only she who could help him, and she trembled at the exciting possibilities a long correspondence would offer. And so without much searching she made her decision, a decision that had begun the moment she started on the letter. Some-how or other she would devise a means of writing to him. She would assume a new persona, and through postal communication, she would give to him what he pleaded. It would not be a deception. As Amy Evans, she was a stifling and strangled companion. In some other guise, unseen, she could loosen. She could per-haps even love. She heard a noise from Stan's room. Even through his closed door, and the closed door of the kitchen, his wheezing rattled like a cracked chapel bell. 'O God,' she whispered, 'let him live long enough to know with certainty that he is deeply loved, and a little longer, and for his own sake, to give that love in return.'

Part Two

It took a bit of planning. There was an address to be decided on; she had no friends whom she could adequately trust to keep a secret. Gwyneth was out of the question. Though she knew everything, this would have to be something that she would never know. She could not retain her Box Number, neither could she give a specific address, and it struck her the half-way house of poste restante would solve the problem. But where? Porthcawl was too close to the fire. She had to bear in mind that a meeting between the correspondents was impossible. Distance could easily excuse it, along with other complications that she would have to manufacture. Cardiff was too far for her to travel to too often—she hoped that their correspondence would be at least a once a week affair. Porth seemed to be the answer. It was a twenty minute bus ride, and Stan would never know she had left Porthcawl. As to their non-meeting, she would devise a plan of postponement, and let time, and the condition of Stan's health, dictate every subsequent move. She would have to disguise her handwriting too, so she took a sheet of paper and tried various styles. After some experiment she decided that the backward slant was the most effective cover-up. And that, coupled with the use of purple ink, would stop up all holes of suspicion. Not that the truth of the matter would ever occur to Stan, but it was such a vast deception that she could afford to take no risks whatever of discovery. What she hoped would turn out to be a prolonged lesson in love, might, if discovered, be seen as an act of terrible pity, mockery even. No. No one would ever know her secret.

It was past midnight. Stan was asleep, but his proximity did not disturb her, and as she wrote she distanced herself further and further from her kitchen, her home, Porthcawl, so that by the time she signed off as Blodwen she was indeed one stranger writing to another. She wrote that she lived in a semi-detached house in Porth, together with her aging mother who needed her constant care. Stan had expressed his preference for a woman just like his sister, so she wrote that she understood Amy very well, and she hastened to add that there was joy in caring for people whom you loved, so that the notion of sacrifice was not a viable proposition. She had stressed how difficult it was for her to leave her mother, so that a meeting between them, for the time being at least, was difficult to arrange, but she hinted at how exciting it would be to get to know each other well simply by correspondence. She told him that Porthcawl was known to her, though it was a long time since she had been there. It had been her childhood summer treat. She, too, knew the rocks and the sands of the bays, though it had much changed, she had heard, since she was a child. She told him about the caves that she'd used as hiding places, and the secret rock pools that she thought were her own inalienable discovery. She wrote to Stan of the things that so often he had begged her to talk about, and in the writing of them she found no discomfort, as if it were another's childhood she revealed. She sent her best regards to Amy, with whom she felt she had much in common. She did not ignore his request for a snap, but it presented certain difficulties. She promised to send one in her next letter. She urged him to reply soon to the poste restante address, explaining with tolerance that her mother was intensely inquisitive, and that she would like their correspondence, should it continue, to be a private one. She added a P.S. 'What about a snap of you, then? That would be nice to put on my bed-side table.' She pictured her little bedroom in Porth, its narrow brass bedstead with Stan's picture beside. Already she was moving into another life, and with a small shock she recognised her own kitchen where most of her life had been spent, and she had a strange sense of being a visitor there.

In the morning she took the bus over to Porth, the first of what were to be many weekly journeys. She posted her letter at the main Post Office, and then went inside to ascertain poste restante arrangements. When all was done she walked slowly through the High Street. She had often passed the photographer's shop on the corner by the bus stop. The windows were full of pictures, of various sizes and for different purposes, with a large invitation to step inside and inspect further possibilities. She obeyed, and with firm resolution, for she knew exactly what she was going to do.

Along the counter ran a range of postcard-size photographs, enlargements of the poly-size squares in the windows. They were a good plain envelope size, and out of the dozen displayed there were at least three which could reliably fit the description of a middle-aged home-maker lady, and one, even, who couldn't possibly be called anything else but Blodwen. That lady lay in the middle of the portrait gallery, which would have been no obstacle in itself, had not the whole display been overlaid with a sheet of glass that made stealing impossible. She looked around the shop for other possibilities. Several portraits stood framed on tables, eminently pinchable, but all were of young brides. Then she saw a picture, more Blodwen than the last. A veritable angel of a home-maker, with sandy coloured hair in soft cheek-touching curls. It was displayed less for its sitter than for its ornate frame, which was a gold arrangement of leaf and flower. Underneath was a notice which proclaimed the shop's framing speciality. 'Made to Order.'

As a child she had stolen frequently. Usually from Woolworths. Chocolate mainly. Never, never rock. Rock, with its inlaid song of her town was sacred, and to steal it would have been like knocking off the church silver. As a child she had stolen quickly, with deft fingers and with little forethought. Now, in her long hesitation, fear gathered, and as she reached out for the picture, ham-fistedly holding open her hold-all and with much public trembling, she knew that she would be caught. It was almost an act of defiance, and when the picture was safely in her bag she looked round the shop for an accuser. She heard its voice ring over the counter, and then saw that it belonged to a little girl, too bloody pretty for Amy's comfort.

'Oo, Mam, look what that old woman done. She took that picture. I seen 'er put it in 'er bag.'

Amy froze. It was not the shock of being caught. That she would deal with later. It was the title by which she'd been summoned, the title in which she would stand in the dock, cowering in her wrinkled years. And of that title, of that accusation, she pleaded a painful innocence. 'I'm not old then,' she shouted back, 'cos that was the plea that held priority. But at that moment, she looked old enough, furrowed with the realisation that though 'thief' was secondary, it was that title she would do time for.

She was surrounded now by hard executive pin-stripe, pointed and patent shoes creaking with capture.

'Will you come this way, Madam?' she heard.

She followed the shoes into a back room, hearing behind her a mixture of sighs, both of pity and righteous indignation.

'I seen 'er,' the little girl repeated, and, 'You don't miss much then, do you, cariad,' from her proud and salivating Mam.

They gave Amy a chair. Ever so polite, like she'd just done them a favour, and though she was trembling violently she began to hope that they would be lenient with her considering her age and her ugliness. She began to cry, fumbling in her bag for a handkerchief she knew would not be there. One of the pin-stripes handed her a box of tissues that lay on the desk, and at the same time he took away the hold-all. A colleague of his made much ceremony of opening the bag, and extracting from it the damning evidence against her. He laid it on the desk.

'What's your name, Madam?' he said.

While he called her Madam, there was hope, still some shred of respect that might preclude her arrest. And she dwelt on this rather than on the question itself. So he had to repeat it, and this time the 'Madam' was not offered.

'Blodwen Pugh,' she said, with not a little pride, and not realising the further traps she might be setting for herself. All she knew was that Amy Evans of Porthcawl was impossible, for come what may, Stan and Gwyneth must never never find out.

'And your address?'

'I beg your pardon?' she asked, playing for time. She knew there would be no takers for a cubby-hole in poste restante. In any case, Porth as well as Porthcawl was out of the question.

'Where do you live?' the pin-stripe was almost shouting.

'In Cardiff,' she said, desperately distancing herself. 'I'm in Porth for the day.'

'Where in Cardiff?'

'Bute Town Road,' she said, as a first instalment, while she milked her brain for the number of the house where Dr Weiner had disposed of her little parlee-voo. 'Eighty-four,' she added brightly, as it came to her, though she had heard that the whole block had been bombed and poor Dr Weiner with it. 'My Mam's very ill,' she added, playing Blodwen to the last. 'Please,' she begged, 'let me go. I'm very, very sorry. I don't know indeed what came over me.'

She couldn't stop crying, burying her face in the already sodden tissue. They moved away from her and she heard their whispering. She saw that they were looking at her, so she held her sad face towards them, so that they could appraise her ugliness, and pity her. They whispered together again, and it is possible that they concluded that with such a face the poor woman had trouble enough.

One of them moved towards her. 'We've decided to let you go,' he said, 'but on condition that you are never seen in this shop again. And you would do well to keep out of the area altogether,' he said.

Her gratitude was overwhelming and she gladly promised what he asked, and would have sworn never to look upon the face of the whole of Porth again had she not committed herself to a box in the Post Office. She almost sailed out of the shop, ignoring the cluster of buyers who were hanging on for the verdict, and the illegally pretty child who repeated yet again, in case any other budding detective took the credit, that it was she and no one else who had shopped her.

She hurried along the High Street and into the first back alley she could find. There was a volcano of shame inside her and she felt the need for its hot release. At the bottom of the lane was an old junk shop. A few kitchen chairs were displayed outside, and she sat on one of them and relived, second by second, her recent mortification. It was a relief to act it out and to savour the luck of her acquittal. She vowed, not that she would never again steal again, for she didn't look upon it as theft—her act had been part of a deed of love contracted with Stan—but that she would never again curse her own ugliness, because possibly for the first time in her life it had been to her advantage, in stirring those pin-stripes to pity.

'You taking a load off your feet, then?' the shopkeeper began collecting his out-of-doors display.

'I was just going to come into the shop,' she said, getting up. 'Having a bit of a rest first.'

'Go on,' he said. 'Sitting's for free. Have a good rest now.'

'I'm obliged,' she said, 'but I'm all right now.' She walked past him into the shop, not wanting to buy anything, but simply to repay his concern with her interest. It was an untidy shop, a treasure trove for 'find' hunters, and the few customers were picking over the piles like panners for gold. On top of a pile of books she saw a large album, and she was attracted to its plush red velvet cover, and the threadbare gold silk on its spine. She picked it up, blowing the dust away, and moved over to an empty corner of the shop to examine it. She glowed as she turned the pages. From cover to cover was Blodwen for legal sale. Blodwen, from her pram to her prime, and not only Blodwen, but her entire family, including a large domineering woman, who might well have turned out to be an ailing and demanding mother. She shut the book quickly. She wanted to save it for closer examination in the privacy of her kitchen when Stan was in bed. Then she could get to know her new-found family; to each one she could attach a story, and altogether they would feed a correspondence that would outlive both of them.

She paid for the book. She would gladly have given the man twice what he asked.

'You don't see a bit of binding like that nowadays,' he said, but it was not craftmanship she was buying, but kin, a brand new exciting lineage, an inheritance of beauty and family feeling. She felt no betrayal of her own Mam and Dad. They had been but obstacles to what was now of prime importance, a rapprochement between herself and her brother. Only Blodwen and her long line of Pughs could bring it about.

On the bus back to Porthcawl she put the book at the bottom of the hold-all and covered it with her handbag, so that she could better resist the temptation of skimming through her new-found family. That could only lead to confusion. She would need time to place each picture in context and relationship. She could freely choose her uncles, aunts, nieces, nephews and ascribe her own opinion to each one of them. She thought it strange that all her life she had been denied choice, and now she had been able to buy it, and much of it, too, for a mere two shillings in a junk shop.

In her excitement she had almost forgotten the incident in the photographer's shop, and she now viewed it as a fortunate necessity that had guided her towards a new family. Until the pretty little girl, her duty done, and her proud Mam, boarded the bus on the outskirts of the town.

'There she is again, Mam,' the little girl shouted.

'The one I seen stealing in the shop,' she added, to make her message clear to the whole bus.

'The cheek of it,' her Mam said, 'travelling around, bold as brass. Sit over here, cariad,' she said, motioning her sickening child to a far seat, away from theft contagion. 'Some people have got no shame,' she said.

All the passengers turned to look at Amy, and Amy, in quick-fire defence, looked around the bus herself, seeking out the accused. This threw the passenger list into some confusion, and the diligent little detective felt called upon again to identify her quarry.

'That old woman,' she said, careful not to point, 'cos her Mam had told her pointing was rude, but at least half a dozen passengers met that description. One of them at this point had reached her stop, so she was obliged to leave the bus, and happily all suspicions fell on her, so that the poor lady was stared after and maligned, as the bus took off again. Mercifully the child and her proud Mam were the next to alight, and Amy avoided their stares as they passed down the aisle. The child hissed as she went by. 'I saw you,' she said. 'You know what you done.'

'That's enough now,' her rotten Mam said at last. 'You don't want to go mixing with the likes of her.'

They got off the bus, and out of the corner of her eye Amy could see them standing on the pavement opposite her seat and staring at her. She waited for the bus to start moving off, then she turned and looked out of the window. She poked out her tongue, so far that it hurt, and put her fingers to her nose at the same time. 'Fuck, fuck,' she mouthed to the little girl and her astonished Mam, and felt vastly better for giving them something to gawp about. She'd had the last word, for the bus drew away before they could retaliate even in gesture.

Yet despite the relief, there was still a sour hangover from the incident in the shop and she dwelt on what might have happened had they decided to make a charge against her. She would have been found out, and Gwyneth and the whole of Porthcawl would mutter that she'd come to a bad end just like her Dad. But her Dad's end had been innocent enough. Sweet-sherried though he was, and trailing sozzled clouds, he'd gone to Abraham's bosom none the less. And she was almost as innocent, for what she had done had been in the name of love, a love through which two lame people could find some foothold. She decided that next Sunday she would go to chapel and sit away from Gwyneth all on her own, and there she would pray for her Dad, her Mam too, though she deserved it less, and thank God for her own acquittal. She would do it alone and aloud, and she'd explain to Gwyneth that it was a secret between God and herself and even Gwyneth would have to be satisfied with that one. She didn't know whether or not she believed in God. Chapel was just somewhere to go on a Sunday. It broke the monotony of a practically house-bound week. As a child, she went there just to curse God for her stubby nose and Stan's irons. Now she would go and thank Him for her acquittal but at the same time she would point out that it was about bloody time He looked her way.

She took the bus right to the terminal, because the walk over the sand dunes was too long and she was impatient to get home and study her new family.

'Amy, is that you?' Stan called as she turned the key in the lock. 'Any post then?' he added. Now it was his turn for waiting.

'Why? You expecting something?' she asked closing the door. 'A billet-doux?' she laughed.

He wheeled his chair out of his room. 'Don't you be so cocky then,' he smiled. 'There's many a girl in Porthcawl would have me, cripple or no.'

She shuddered. To read the word in his letter had been shock enough. Now to hear it drop from his lips, as lightly as a crumb from her sponge cake, irritated her as much, and she would have liked to sweep it up with her dust-pan so that it was all nice and tidy as it had been before. 'Don't you go using those terrible words now,' she said.

'Well it's true, isn't it? Time you and me faced the facts, Amy. That's what I am. There's no gainsaying. A cripple. Say it, Amy.' He was laughing. 'Say it after me. A cripple.' In no time the carpet would be covered with his ejaculation. A permanent stain that no amount of cleaning up after him would remove.

'Well, if that's what you like to think,' she said, 'that's what you are. What you said.'

'Well say it then,' he challenged her.

'All right. If you want it, Stan Evans, you can have it. You're a cripple,' she shouted, and her anger excited her to repeat it. 'A cripple. Always was. Always will be.'

Stan laughed, frantically wheeling his chair around and around her. He was toasting the loud publication of his infirmity, and she in turn lifted her glass too. 'And I'm an old maid,' she shouted, dancing round him.

'Old maid Amy Evans,' he called back, 'Always was, always will be.'

So together they celebrated their separate disorders, and together, with their approved labellings of each other, they felt the beginnings of liberation. Stan swivelled his chair around her, and she waltzed to his movement. Slowly their dance took on an air of formality.

She raised her head, crowing her status aloud, while he bowed his in acknowledgment. And then it was his turn. So they trumpeted each other like the courtship dance of two aging penguins with beating hearts and frayed plumage. Then they stopped and stared at each other, knowing that something had happened between them and not totally understanding it, but knowing for certainty that it was a turning point for both of them.

'I'll make an apple pie,' Amy said, turning away and off-setting the embarrassment for them both. 'We'll have it for our supper.'

*   *   *

She kept the album hidden. In the excitement of looking for a good hiding place she realised that, for the first time in her life, she had a secret, and that it was because everything about herself was known that life had been so monotonous. Now she harboured a secret that she wanted no one to share, a secret that in time and correspondence would grow into a code, with hidden ciphers of kin, of aunts, uncles and the like, a whole secret charter of family. For it was all there, for her taking and her holding. She ran her hand over the soft red leather cover. Blodwen's mother, the ailing one, must have bought it in the very beginning, or perhaps it was a present from her husband, now long dead. She looked at his picture, seeking a clue of how he had died. He was a strong and healthy looking man, and each picture of him, whether alone or with his family, formally or on holiday, showed the grand capacity for enjoyment, and Amy concluded that, failing accident, such a man could only have died from old and contented age. She named him Ivor, for that was how he looked, the teddy bear uncle of her childhood.

Blodwen's Mam was harder to fathom. The fact that she was still alive inhibited conjecture, but from her pictures it was obvious that she was born to rule, and was no doubt ruling still in the semi-detached in Porth. Amy didn't like her very much, and for some reason that Amy didn't want to understand the old lady answered quite naturally to the name of Gwyneth. Having decided on her parentage, she closed the book. She wanted to ration herself with the enjoyment it offered. Next time she would deal with her brothers and sisters, and afterwards with her more distant kin. She would leave Blodwen, whom she loved most, to the last, until she was well acquainted with her overall context. Then, over the pages, she would learn to know her, and parts of that knowledge she would share with Stan.

She heard him singing in his room. It was an old Welsh hymn, a mournful tune, that was inserted into the chapel service after a disaster at the pit. He sang it loudly and with praise, with the noble timbre of lament which is close to joy. He sang rarely nowadays, for despite a good tenor voice he had hardly used it since the Porthcawl Male Voice Choir had disbanded. She remembered the annual performances of the Messiah, and how her heart beat through the overture. Then when it was done, a voice, distant and desolate as a ghost's echoed through the cold church hall. Three notes on a descending scale. 'Comfort ye.' The audience, those who were new to the form, would sniff out the source of that urgent cry, scanning the rows of the seated choir for a single mouth that moved. You could tell, by their sighs, when they had tracked it down to the wheel-chair. Then they would lean back and marvel, not so much at the voice, for good tenors were two a penny in the Welsh valleys, but that one, so handicapped, could enjoin them to comfort. In those days, his voice had been extraordinarily powerful, as if the strength, forbidden his lower body, had defiantly proclaimed itself in his chest. But now, over-burdened, it threatened to fail him. So it was only rarely now that he sang, and somehow its muted quality moved her even more than it had in the church hall days.

Amy listened until the hymn was finished, and then he started almost immediately on 'All Through The Night'. She knew that the 'Ash Grove' would follow and 'The Minstrel Boy' after that, for he was going through the community song book that her Dad had bought with his cigarette coupons. Sometimes on a Sunday when they were small, her Dad would thump out the accompaniment on the piano in the parlour. They had sold the piano to make room for a television set, but Amy remembered it in detail. Pleyel it was called, in scrolled gold letters and there was fretwork in the front with frayed rose silk trellised behind. On each side was a brass candlestick. Amy's sole contribution to the musical life of the house was to polish these brass holders till you could see your distorted face in them. Though once her Dad had tried to teach her to play. She could always find middle C and D, for their ivories were discoloured, and often when she was sad she would play them one after the other, and the tune was mournful as if the keys had turned blue from sadness. But her Dad played beautiful, she remembered, and he would sing too, descanting Stan. Sometimes her Mam would interfere with an off-key soprano, but nobody said anything because all of them knew that it was their Mam's job to go and spoil everything.

Amy listened, as the minstrel boy to the war had gone. It was but the fourth song in a book of a hundred, enough notes to tide him over till the post came and came again. She wondered whether it ever passed through his mind that no letter would come, as she herself had feared for so many endless days. Now those days seemed to her in a distant past, in another life almost, days consumed one after the other in reliable monotony.

When she'd woken up that morning, her letter to Stan safely in the post, she had almost leapt from her bed, and only when putting on her slippers did she realise that she had omitted to perform a ritual of years-of-mornings standing, that of clasping her nose as the alarm bell woke her. Even as a child she had done it, as automatically as most children would have rubbed sleep from the eye. But for Amy, every morning brought the hope that the stubby nose had grown, that some new shape had asserted itself during her sleep that would pass muster as an acceptable breathing organ. She had long since given up hope of nocturnal metamorphosis, but the gesture had become automatic, and as she put on her slippers that morning she had a sense of having forgotten something. It was only now that she realised that a time-honoured rite had proved itself superfluous.

Even though she knew that there would be no post for her, she was excited at the thought of the arrival of her letter to Stan. She knew that she could not be disappointed and she smiled with approval as she saw it lying in the box as she went down the stairs to the kitchen. She picked it up and looked at her purple back-slanting hand. Blodwen's hand it was, neat and precise, generously planted with commas, and the neat capital letters of GLAM, short for Glamorgan, that was itself printed in brackets at the bottom of the envelope. A letter that could not on any account go astray. Stan would appreciate that.

She tried to be off-hand about it, and when she brought in his tea she threw it indifferently on to the bed. 'Letter for you,' she said, and she went quickly from the room in case he opened it in front of her. He received letters seldom. Normally she would have asked him who it was from, and her omission to do so on this occasion might arouse his suspicion. She decided to ask him at breakfast, without showing too much interest. She listened outside his door, but she heard no rustle of paper. He must be savouring the look of the envelope, hoarding his little treat. She went back into the kitchen and went over in her mind what she had written him, reading it with him as it were, but it took him longer it seemed, for it was some time before he came to breakfast. She felt suddenly shy of him. She turned to the sink and said quickly, 'You got a letter then.' She felt herself blushing.

'It was about a stamp catalogue,' he said. 'There's a new issue.'

She busied herself at the sink for she was still not ready to look at him. She dared not risk blushing or giggling in front of him, or giving any sign that she did not believe him. 'Going to send off for it, then?' she said to the dishes in the sink.

'Yes,' he said. 'It's an address in Porth. Some woman. Blodwen Pugh. She's started up her own business. Stamp bulletins. Once a week, she says.'

She marvelled at the speed and feasibility of his cover. He had also given her a clue as to the rhythm of their correspondence. It was to be a once-weekly affair, so she could time her journeys to Porth accordingly.

'Oh it's stuffy in here this morning,' she said, giving some explanation for her red face, and she sat down at the table to eat with him. 'That was nice, your singing yesterday. Wonder what happened to the community song book?'

'Got lost, I suppose,' he said with little interest.

'You used to sing so beautiful,' she said. 'Remember the Messiah every Christmas?'

'Yes,' he said, and that was all, because he didn't need her any more for memory sharing. He was keeping it all for Blodwen.

Amy was satisfied, and she was glad when Gwyneth arrived, rather later than usual, with the bread. Without taking off her coat she leaned over Stan to reach for the bread knife, and in so doing, she let out a little squeak.

'Oo, there's disgusting,' she said, turning to Stan, and it was only after her automatic verbal response that she realised what had caused it. It had been many, many years since poor Gwyneth had been pinched on her bottom, and the event was shock enough. But that it should have been done by Stan, stealthily, under the table, almost, was far beyond her understanding. She sat down to recover herself. 'Stan Evans,' she said. 'After all these years, I don't know what's come over you.'

'What's the matter?' Amy said, guessing full well what had happened, but wanting to savour the words of it.

'I pinched her bum,' Stan said proudly, and his choice of word did not improve matters for Gwyneth.

'Disgusting,' she muttered again, as if the word were her wand of exorcism.

'Pinched her bum, I did,' Stan said again, and the repeat was Amy's share. Amy looked at Stan and together they burst out laughing, and poor Gwyneth squirmed with the betrayal.

'I don't see the joke myself,' she said on her dignity,

and with half a mind to wrap up the bread and take it away. 'Bad enough to do it, I would say. Downright vulgar to put it into words.'

'Oh come on, Gwyneth girl,' Amy said. 'It's only a joke. Stan will have his bit of fun.'

'Well, he's never done it before,' Gwyneth said, and Amy had to agree with her, though wondering less than Gwyneth what had come over him.

'Then I shall have to make up for lost time, shan't I?' Stan said, and losing not a moment of it he pinched her again, this time on her ribs and perilously close to her breast.

Gwyneth got up, dreading what target he would choose next and she moved to the top of the table to get out of the line of fire.

'It's only a bit of fun,' Amy said again to appease, but inwardly she was disturbed at the effect just one single letter had had on him. She wondered to what lengths he would go as the correspondence proceeded, and whether Gwyneth would continue to come with the daily bread. Although she liked Stan in this mood, for it excited her too, she did not wish to lose Gwyneth as a friend. If only Gwyneth would relax and play along with Stan, they might make a happy threesome. Amy passed her the bread knife, which gave Gwyneth something to do instead of sitting there squirming and wondering where to put her hands. She cut the bread in silence, moving each slice to her side, out of Stan's reach, to punish him. But quickly he wheeled his chair to the top of the table, manoeuvring it behind her, so that he could put his arms around her and take the bread at the same time. It was too much for Gwyneth, and she burst into tears.

'Duw, I'm sorry, then,' Stan said with genuine regret, and he put out his hand to place it on her shoulder. But he thought better of it. Gwyneth had by now made it quite clear that she was, in every part of her, untouchable.

Amy did her best to comfort her. 'It's not fair, Stan,' she said, 'teasing our Gwyneth like that. It's only a tease, Gwyneth,' she said. 'You don't have to take exception. He was only being friendly.' It occurred to her that she was talking about Stan as if he were a pet dog, and she couldn't help thinking that Gwyneth was overdoing it a bit with her blubbering. 'Come on, now. The bread's still warm,' she said, 'and there's some plum jam to go with it.'

'My best friends,' Gwyneth blubbered, shivering with the after-sense of all that touching. Amy felt profoundly sorry for her. Gwyneth, who all her life had protected herself from what she most desired, had now grown wholly unstirrable. She was weeping for that, Amy knew, for the realisation of all that she had lost out on, for a frigidity excused over the years, by knowing everything.

'We're still your best friends,' Stan said, wheeling his chair back to his place. 'Would only do that sort of thing with your best friend.'

'But you never did it before,' she whimpered. 'In all these years. My *only* friends,' she said, a little more honest this time. 'I come to bring a bit of home-baked bread, and what do I find? I'm telling you,' she said. 'An orgy.'

'But he only pinched your behind,' Amy said, wondering how much of their correspondence Gwyneth could survive. If only one letter from Blodwen prompted bum-pinching, whatever would he graduate to over the weeks. Gwyneth was right. There might come a time when her term 'orgy' would be well-founded, and Amy thrilled with such a possibility. 'Pass the bread, will you then, Gwyneth,' she said. 'It'll be nice with a bit of home-made jam.' She wanted to get back on an even keel, to the safe monotony of their morning dialogue. There had been enough deviation.

Gwyneth responded. 'Don't be greedy now,' she said, as Stan stretched out his hand. She, too, was glad of harbour. Thereafter it was the same as it had always been, superficially at least, with non-conversation of non-events, speculation on the weather, the rising cost of living, and how soon Porthcawl, and with it the rest of the country, would go to the dogs. 'Disgusting,' Gwyneth said, as one would say Amen, and she rose from the table to take her leave. She didn't pat Stan on the head as she went. Suddenly he had become too old for that sort of thing. She sidled past him, using her shopping bag as a shield.

'Will we see you tomorrow, then?' Amy said, though the question had never been necessary before.

'If you can behave yourselves,' Gwyneth said. 'The last thing I want is to break a friendship.'

There was no doubt in anyone's mind that Gwyneth would come in the morning. And the next day, and the next. She was postulating the notion of friendship as a licence that legalised everything. Gwyneth, tight-lipped and bottomed, would be coming back for more.

When she had gone, they looked at each other, their first declaration of conspiracy. They heard a screech of gulls over the bay. 'There's a fine flock, then,' Stan said, wheeling himself over to the window.

It was the first time in many years that he'd given a hint of even noticing them. Amy looked at him, hunched in his chair, his eyes blazing. A great and rude appetite for life had suddenly assaulted his old age and frailty, and she feared that his time and his strength would run their stubborn course before it could be satisfied.

* * *

She took the first morning bus to Porth. She would go straight to the Post Office—she knew Stan had written, because he'd told her he'd sent off for his catalogue when he'd spent the day with Gwyneth—and she would collect her letter and take the first bus back. She would not be able to avoid the photograph shop, but she would hurry past it on the other side of the road, her head bowed, in case anyone remembered her face.

There was a queue at the poste restante counter, which did not please her, and she kept fumbling in her bag, her face hidden. She wondered why so many people used the service, and what secrets they were hiding in their cubby-holes. None of them looked in need of an alias, but neither, she supposed, did she. They were possibly wondering too what she was doing there, and she was suddenly overcome with a sharp curiosity to know a little of their business.

'Waiting for poste restante, then?' she said to the lady in front of her.

She nodded. 'Bit of a queue this morning,' she said. 'Better to come in the afternoon.' She was Welsh and willing.

'Of course,' she added, 'could be waiting for nothing.'

'D'you come here often?' Amy said, leading her on.

'Every week,' she said. 'It's my husband you see,' she went on chattily, 'if he knew I was still in touch with our Margaret, well, he'd kill me. That he would. No doubt about it.'

'What she do, then?' Amy asked without prying, for the woman was obviously eager to share her burden.

'Married an Englishman,' she said.

'That's not so terrible.'

'Hit the roof he did. Threw her out. Our only child, would you believe. I begged him, and he threatened to throw me out with her. He's a good man, really, my Emrys. But a temper. I tell you, you don't want to be around when he's crossed. Wounded he was in the war you see. The first one. Got a metal plate in his head. I'm sure that's the reason, 'cos he's a gentle man really, but sometimes, you see, he can't control it. He hasn't clapped eyes on our Margaret since, ten years it is now.'

'Do you ever see her then?' Amy asked.

'Oh yes,' the woman whispered. 'I'm her mother, d'you see. She's in Cardiff, and sometimes we meet in Bridgend like, in a tea-shop, but she writes to me once a week. She's a good girl, our Margaret. If he ever found out about it, this Post Office business, I mean, or the meetings, he'd kill me. I'm not telling you a word of a lie. Why, I can't even mention her name in the house. Still, he's a good man,' she insisted again. 'Just can't abide the English. Mind you, I'm not a one for the English myself, but there's good and bad.'

Amy nodded. The queue moved forward a little, and a small lady, neatly dressed, was peering through the grille. The clerk looked in the box, and shook his head. The other clerks were watching him, and when the lady turned away from the grille, he shared with the others a shrug of understanding.

'They all know her,' Amy's companion said. 'She's been coming every week for God knows how long. Waiting for a letter from her husband. She's not quite right in the head like, 'cos her husband was killed in the war, the last one that is, not the one that gave my Emrys his wound—the lady was anxious to avoid a confusion of hostilities—yet every week she comes, regular as a clock, like, 'cos it was a Thursday, like today, that she collected his letter when he wrote from his camp. Poor soul. They know her here, but every week when she comes, they look in the cubby-hole, like they expected something to be there. There's a lot of trouble about,' the woman added, and without pausing for breath she said, 'And why is it, if you don't mind me asking, I'm not a one given to prying, but why are you here?'

After her generous offerings the lady was entitled to some story in return. 'It's not for me,' Amy said quickly, with the time-honoured alibi of a liar. 'It's for my friend. She's looking for a house to buy, and at present she has no proper address. Staying with me, she is, for the time being. Blodwen, her name is,' Amy said chattily. 'Blodwen Pugh. Such a nice woman.'

The queue moved forward. 'I hate to see them disappointed,' the woman said, as a gentleman turned empty-handed from the grille. 'Not seen him here before. I know most of them though. Get to know them over the years, like. Like going to the launderette in a way,' she mused, and she was happy to consider the similarities in silence for a while. She was close to her turn. 'I get a bit nervous,' she confided to Amy, 'just in case there's nothing for me. But she's a good girl, is our Margaret. If there's no letter, you can take it from me, there's a very good reason. Mrs Williams,' she said when she reached the grille. 'B. Williams. B for Beryl.' Though the clerk knew her well, she wanted no oversight. He went to the row of boxes, and Amy prayed that Margaret had written.

'Your usual, then,' the man said, turning back with a letter in his hand. 'And don't worry, Mrs Williams, I shan't tell a soul. She's a good girl, your Margaret, whatever anyone says.'

So they all knew about it, except perhaps Mr Williams, and possibly he knew about it too, but found it easier to ignore. Amy wondered whether over the weeks they would speculate about her too.

'I'll see you again, no doubt,' Mrs Williams said, clutching her letter. 'I hope your friend finds satisfaction.'

Amy found herself at the grille. She didn't know the form, and the clerk didn't help her. 'I . . . I've come for a letter,' she stammered.

The clerk looked her over. Sometimes it took years to get to know another's business. There were lots of clues, the postmark on the envelope, the regularity of collection, and the general demeanour of the recipient. This one stammered. She obviously had something to hide. He hoped she'd be a regular, so that he could get to know her story.

'Name please,' he said.

'Pugh,' she said. 'Blodwen Pugh.'

'Blodwen Pugh, is it?' he said loudly, for the benefit of the rest of the staff, just in case she should come in one day when he was off-duty.

'Mrs?' he asked doubtfully.

'Miss,' she confessed, and felt she should apologise for it.

'Miss Blodwen Pugh,' he repeated. 'Let's see if we have something for you, Madam.' He went over to the holes. Amy watched him, trembling. He ran his fingers over the whole alphabet, teasing her. She had no doubt a letter was there, and why couldn't he look in 'P' and be done with it. Which he finally did. He took out the envelope and held it high, noting the Porthcawl postmark, and the undoubtedly masculine hand. 'Miss Pugh,' he announced, and he brought it with ceremony to the counter. 'Glad not to disappoint you, Madam,' he said.

She took the letter with shaking fingers, not looking at him.

'See you again, Madam?'

'Thank you,' she said. She wasn't giving anything away. The clerk shrugged and turned to the next applicant.

'Mr Davies,' he said, 'bound to be one this week. What is it now? Three weeks since your Dai wrote? You can tell him from me, he's a lazy scoundrel.'

Amy hurried out of the Post Office and along the High Street. She crossed the road before the photographer's shop and hurried past on the opposite side. There was a queue at the bus stop and while she waited she put Stan's letter into her bag and stuffed it into the hold-all. She was a little disturbed by the over-friendliness of the clerk at the Post Office, and her mood was not improved by the sound of a painfully familiar voice.

'Oo look, Mam, there's that woman. You know, Mam. Look now Mam,' the child insisted.

They both stopped and stared at her. Mindful of the tail-end of their last encounter, they had a score to settle, but short of a dialogue, which the woman wouldn't lower herself to, there was only gesture, and the place was too public for that, and would have appeared unsolicited, and thus reflect poorly on herself. But she had to do something. So she dragged her child over to the bus queue, sliding past Amy, so that she almost grazed her, and whispered "thief" into her ear, spitting at the same time. Amy refrained from wiping her face until the woman was gone, and the hate welled up in her like a fever. She fingered Stan's letter in her bag. It was a fantasy, she knew, but she had to make it real enough to cling to. She was slowly overcome by the futility of her pursuit, that, correspondence or not, her ugliness could only get uglier, her loneliness more acute. But at least, she consoled herself, the deception was doing something for Stan. When the time would come for Dr Rhys to pronounce his final verdict, and, with due respect to his own father who had predicted it some fifty years ago, adding that it was to be expected, he would be sentencing a man who had known a deep and sustaining love, that could express itself only in anonymity. The memory that would be docked when he died would not be of his Mam's honeyed coddling, but of the weekly postal missive in purple ink, and back-slanting hand.

'Whatever am I going to do with his chair?' she thought to herself, the handrails on the bed and bath, and all the iron paraphernalia of his handicap. Duw, there'll be some cleaning up to do after him, but, by God, the thought exploded inside her, there'll be no cleaning up to do after him, and no trifle on a Sunday and no apple pie for treats, and just her and Gwyneth breaking the morning bread. She looked again at the letter. She would read it as soon as she got home, and it would make it all better. When Stan died, as she knew he must, she would, unlike Gwyneth, still have her pen pal for company, and as she sat in the bus she held on to this thought, totally unaware of her own confusion.

Stan was out when she got home—his Gwyneth day. So she had the house to herself, with no fear of witness to her trembling anticipation. She was pleasantly ashamed of her excitement; the reading of love letters belonged to the map of adolescence. She had missed out on it then, yet she could not imagine that the excitement of a teenager on the receipt of her first throbbing missive could have been more acute than hers. She opened all the doors of the house so that she would be warned of any disturbing movement, though she could positively expect none, and then she sat at the kitchen table staring at the letter. Unlike a teenager she knew, from her many and sad years' experience, that moments like this were to be savoured to their full, for they were not likely to be many more. So she was content to sit and stare at the letter, for that was part of the enjoyment too. Then when her knees had ceased their trembling, and her heart-beat was out of her hearing, she prised the letter open, careful not to disturb the triangle of its sealing. As she took the letter out, a photograph dropped from the fold. Half of it had been cut off and scissored in such a way as to precisely define the outline of Stan in his chair. Even the shape of his head was cut with respect to every curl. One shoulder had been slightly overtrimmed but apart from that tiny excess, it was a perfect piece of patterning, a miniature, tailored to fit into a locket. He had obviously had that in mind, for nestling in another fold of the letter was one of his curls.

Her knees began to tremble again. She had a locket. It had been her Mam's, and her Dad had gently unclasped it from her rigid neck when she had died. He had given it to Amy. 'You have it love,' he had whispered. 'I gave it to her when we were wed.' Amy was curious as to her Mam's love-object, and though it should have been her Dad she did not expect to find his likeness inside. And when she prised the gold case open, she was not surprised to find it empty. It was a fraud, and Amy wouldn't wear it, so she put it away with little hope that it would ever be tenanted. Now she went quickly to her bedroom and unlocked the small drawer of the dressing-table. The locket looked larger than she remembered it. On her Mam's neck, it was a mean small thing, hiding its empty shame under her jumper. Now she would fill it and wear it proudly, and Stan would notice it with surprise and without assumption.

She laid the photograph on the table, and set the curl so that it covered the wheel chair. That way it would fit the locket nicely. She looked again at the photograph, trying to remember when it was taken. Stan looked much as he did today, so it must have been a recent one. Then she noticed that Stan was holding a book in his hand, and she saw the background of the picture in sudden and painful detail.

It had been taken a few years ago, in the forecourt of the chapel, when Huw's daughter Dilys had got married. And the other half of the photograph, that which Stan had so carefully cut away, was of herself, standing by his chair after the ceremony. It had not been a good one of her anyway. She had been more than miserable on that day. Gwyneth had been showing off for weeks before, playing one-upmanship with the continuity of the Price line. Amy did not need to be reminded that when she and Stan were gone the Evans would be no more. But for weeks before the wedding, Gwyneth had hinted at it with her daily bread, so that Amy had been driven to a seething envy that she could barely contain. She was not looking forward to the wedding, but there was no question of not attending. She and Stan were guests of honour, being the Price's oldest friends, and their absence, short of dire illness, could only be construed as jealousy. Amy dared to hope that perhaps Stan would have an off-day. He had them often enough, so she was not wishing him ill, but she prayed that his next bad turn would respect convenient timing. But on the morning of the wedding he was fit and raring to go. He seldom had such a treat in his life, and he looked forward to meeting old friends and sharing other people's joy. So she dragged on a silk dress, bought years before for a Salvation Army garden party, and a wilted flower hat, and Stan looked at her and refrained from comment. It was the kindest thing he could do. He himself wore his only suit, that had fitted him forever, the button-hole sporting a white carnation that Gwyneth had sent over that breadless morning. She sat through the ceremony, a lump in her throat.

'Cheer up,' Gwyneth said beside her.

'Always want to cry at weddings,' Amy said, able then with her alibi to burst into tears for all the ugliness and disorder that had halted the Evans line. She looked a fair eye-sore when they all came out of chapel, and Gwyneth had insisted that Amy pose for her picture by Stan's chair. Gwyneth stood to one side, with Huw, and she eyed them both as if they were her property, while the photographer twiddled his lens.

'Are you ready now?' he said, and Amy overheard Gwyneth tell her brother, 'Pity for them both,' she said. And then the camera clicked, so it was just as well Stan had discarded her, and with her all the bitterness and misery that he must have felt partly responsible for.

But now she didn't mind all that, and she picked up the photograph and the curl and locked them together in the case. Then she fastened the chain around her neck. She spread the letter open. There were six pages of it, written in a careful hand. She could see how frequently the pen had been dipped—Stan had an aversion to biros—for the ink-thickness overall was uneven. For his birthday she would buy him a fountain pen, she thought, and have him over to Porth for tea and to meet her ailing mother. 'What am I thinking?' she thought, but she enjoyed the confusion, and had no wish to sort it out for herself. So she started to read the letter straight away, so that the fantasy, if that was what it was, could be fed.

'Dear Blodwen,' she read. 'There's nice it is to know your name. It reminds me of harps. There was a woman once, my teacher she was, who played the harp lovely. Miss Griffiths she was called, but I found out at a concert that her name was Blodwen, because it was written in the programme. Naturally I always called her Miss Griffiths, but when I listen to the harp, it is Blodwen I think of, and that is a pleasant thought, so I'm glad you have that name. What a lot we have in common then, with sandy beaches and rocks and things. And you have things in common with my sister too, looking after an ailing person like you do. We are made for each other, it seems to me. (I can see you blushing, Blod.) I try to imagine what it is you look like. Will you send me a snap? I have a picture of you in my thoughts like, and I know you are right lovely. Shall I tell you what I think you look like? I'll leave out the face, 'cos I know for certain that's pretty. It's your body I dwell on Blodwen, and if my pen is shaky like, it is because I am trembling with the thought of it. The thought of your big cosy bosoms that I would like to lie between. Duw. Oh Blod, wouldn't that be lovely.'

Amy covered the page with her hand. It was a letter you had to rest from, an instalment letter, else desire explode inside you. She was quite unfamiliar with the tinglings in her body, and unashamed too, of her joy of them. The future dazzled her with its promise of such lasting bliss, for the letter could be read over and over and for ever, without any warning of thrill. She noticed how heavily she was breathing, how her heart pumped with astonishment, and she went to the window to calm herself with the sight of the sea. A single and indifferent gull flew over the bay, as if nothing at all had changed below. She returned to the letter for reassurance.

'But enough of that,' Stan went on. He had somehow sensed her threshold and now he would give her words for her recovery.

'Yesterday I went to the pier with my friend Gwyneth. She's a friend of the family really, and she takes me out once a week to give our Amy a bit of a breather. The band was playing, and there was a new trombonist, who's just settled in Porthcawl, so I'm given to understand. Duw, can he blow, Blodwen. I sat and watched him while he was giving a solo. A rendering of The Ash Grove it was. And the veins were bursting in his neck almost, and I bet you his bowels were stretching too, and I had a vision like, of him blowing himself out, piece by piece, all his veins and arteries, his intestines, and then stomping on them all as if they were sand-dumplings, and blowing all the time, till he blew out his heart that plopped over the jetty into the sea. Duw Blodwen, it was lovely.'

Amy covered the page again. Her body boiled. Somehow, in the story of the hornblower, there was more titillation than in his earlier speculations about her figure. She wondered whether the writing of such words gave Stan the same tremblings. She had to go to the window again, and as she cooled, she realised how, after so many years, and at such close proximity, how little she knew her brother. It was truly a stranger who was writing to her and the correspondence was a fantasy no longer. She went back to the letter, and a new paragraph. He must now, she hoped, give her some relief, some words to mark time, some thought to still the curling brew inside her.

'On the way back from the pier,' he wrote, 'Gwyneth wheeled me along the beach. It was so quiet there.

No one had been since the tide went out, and I was sorry in a way that the wheels of my chair made marks on the smooth oily sand. It was like a disturbance of nature like, and when I think of it, so am I, a cripple like I am in my chair. But I thought to myself, the sea will come in and cover the marks again, and mend the wounds on the sand, like no incoming tide will heal mine. So after a bit, I didn't mind about the wheels and it was lovely to listen to the gulls screeching, and to breathe the salt spray of the sea. Oh I wish I could see you Blodwen, and we could go down to the sea together, like we were children again. Duw, that would be lovely. Oh, I look forward to your next letter. There's so much I want to tell you about, like when I was in school and my Mam and Dad were alive. But I don't wish to bore you any more so I will close now, and will wait with patience till you write. Yours sincerely, Stan. P.S. Blodwen, tell me what you *think* of my letter. Is it *all right* for me to be writing in this manner? It's important what you *think*. Do you *like* it? That's what I want to know.'

Amy folded the letter. She was calm now. His last paragraph had rested her. His P.S. had asked for her forgiveness of his style, if that was in order, and if not, for her permission for him to continue in the same vein. Not only would she give it to him, she would return his style too. Together they would explore the perilous and dark corridors of joy which, all their lives, their each and separate disorders had forbidden. So she wrote to him at once, while his fire still kindled inside her.

She wrote to him of her body, of Blodwen's warm and welcoming flesh, and with loud and tidal words she stoked his fires. As she wrote she understood that there was equal pleasure in giving as in receiving, and that both she and Stan would grow fulsome and blessed in their verbal exchange. She told him of her summer days in Porthcawl, of her Dad who taught her to swim, of her uncle who was always playing tricks. She wrote about Tommy and the ventriloquist and she asked if he ever thought the doll was real. She enclosed a photograph of herself, and added what had now become an obligatory P.S. 'I hope the snap is to your satisfaction. Also the lock of hair.'

She wrote it down though she knew it presented certain problems. Her straggly locks were no love tokens. But a strand of hair could be doctored a little. She cut a small piece from the nape where it was thickest, and she heated an old pair of curling tongs her Mam had once used. Holding one end between her fingers, she carefully curled the other. But the tongs were too hot, and all she succeeded in doing was filling the kitchen with the acrid smell of burnt hair. She tried again, with a smaller lock this time—her hair was not so abundant that she could be extravagant with it—and she managed to achieve a curl half way between a comma and a stroke. She knew it would not travel well. She curled it into a hairclip, but that looked much too common. So she unclipped it and sprayed it with cologne. Though straight it had a touch of class, and confident she sealed the envelope. Then she took a red ribbon from her work-box and wrapped it round the two letters she had received from Stan. These she locked into her dressing-table drawer. Her preparations were complete. She felt more than ready to travel.

*   *   *

Over the weeks, the correspondence grew more and more ardent. Gwyneth came with the daily bread, her

119

body black and blue. On the days when a letter arrived, Stan would dole out an extra ration of teasing, and though she still complained she no longer dodged the line of fire. The summer had begun. It had arrived without transition. It was suddenly mid-summer hot, and the sandy beach looked like a desert.

'Let's have a picnic,' Stan said. 'We can go down to the bay. There'll be no one there in the middle of the week. We can take our lunch.'

He looked from one woman to the other. To picnic in the middle of the week was indeed an extravagance, but he looked so excited at the prospect, and so pleading, that it was difficult to deny him.

'Why not then?' Amy said. 'I shall make us lunch. Lucky for us we've got a chicken. You've got someone to look after the shop, Gwyneth. Go back quick now, and make arrangements.'

Gwyneth was slightly nervous at the idea, but Stan had only to nudge her arm playfully for her to be won over. 'I'll make us a trifle,' she said. 'I'll be back within the hour.'

'And I shall bring the sherry bottle,' Amy said. They might as well go the whole way. 'What are we doing then, Stan?' she said when Gwyneth had gone.

'Celebrating we are,' he said.

'Whose birthday is it then?'

'It must be somebody's,' he said.

'Go on, Stan, you're daft.'

'No harm in being daft,' he said. 'Should be daft more often.'

'You'll need an extra pullover,' Amy said. 'Bound to be chilly in the open. And I'll go and change myself.'

As she said it, she knew that the time was ripe; trouser-ripe, in fact, and she hurried to her room to christen her trousseau. It lay tissue-wrapped in her bottom drawer, the only item in her collection. She had peppered it with lavender-bags and moth-balls, and she held the cloth lovingly to her stubby nose which, after so many years, had lately ceased to trouble her. Already they smelt of camphorated history, the odour of empty chiffoniers. It didn't trouble her. By the ancestral smell of them Stan might think that they were an old pair that she had never worn, and she didn't want to give the impression that she had bought something new without an occasion. Though a picnic was a rare event in their lives nowadays, she didn't want to make a production of it. Nor even a treat. There was no reason why picnics should not be part of a summer routine, and trousers likewise.

She was nervous of putting them on. Over all the weeks, while they had been lying in the drawer, she had thought of them, in her shopping expeditions, in the poste restante at Porth, at meals with Stan; she had tried them on over and over again, and each time she was slimmer. Each time her legs were longer, her waist smaller. Now, with much effort, she willed herself back to the changing-room mirror in the shop, and tried to find it as beautiful. She fixed her mind on that true reflection as she drew them on, each leg singly, and as she screwed her eyes tight she willed that they would parcel her without protest. She patted them fondly when their work was done, and she sought out a blouse that would do them justice. She finally settled on an old cardigan. Her choice was deliberate. She wanted something worn and familiar, that would hold Stan's thankful eye should the trousers disturb him. She wanted to wait in her room till Gwyneth arrived, to protect her trousers from a double début, so she paced up and down, practising a trousered walk, a trousered stand, a trousered sitting, trying to acquire a trouser-talent that man owned simply by nature. By the time Gwyneth rang the bell, she had exhausted herself.

'Coming,' she shouted. She tried a casual slouching down the stairs—trousers somehow called for an offhand gait—and as she reached the front door she realised that Gwyneth would be harder to face than Stan. That Gwyneth might laugh at her, or giggle with little effort to hide it, and she wished that Stan would wheel his chair into the hall to support her. She put a smile on her face, allowing for a joke to be made of her get up, a joke she would willingly share. When she opened the door and saw Gwyneth standing there, French-tailored too by Pugh's on the pier, though in green and two sizes smaller, she felt a mixture of relief and irritation. On the one hand it was a comfort that two of them were in fancy dress, but on the other lay an element of scene stealing. Moreover she had to admit to herself that Gwyneth was the better model. What thoughts were passing through Gwyneth's mind she couldn't tell, though 'disgusting' must have been one of them. Amy held on to her smile.

'Duw mun,' they both said to each other at the same time.

'There's a sly one you are,' Amy said. 'Going to Pugh's on the quiet.'

'Same to you then,' Gwyneth said. 'There's disgusting we are.'

Amy laughed. 'Speak for yourself,' she said, holding on to the joke they were forced to make of themselves. 'Suits you though,' Amy added generously.

'You don't look too bad yourself. Got to admit it, Amy, they're comfy. Can't think why we haven't done it before. I'll buy another pair if you will. A colour you need, Amy. Something bright. Red like. So they'll see you coming,' she laughed.

'Stan'll have a blue fit,' Amy said. 'Stan,' she called, relieving Gwyneth of her trifle and ushering her into the kitchen. From the back Gwyneth looked like a house, and Amy was glad until she wondered what quarters her own rear resembled. But black, she knew, diminished, and that was reassuring.

Stan was still in his room. 'Come on then,' Gwyneth shouted, anxious for his verdict. Amy positioned herself behind the table, preparing the hamper. But when they heard Stan's chair creaking down the hall, Gwyneth too had cold feet and stood herself behind Amy, so that all he saw when he wheeled himself into the kitchen was their familiar cardigan tops. He too had joined the parade. His contribution was a white panama hat that their Dad had bought specially to referee the annual bowls match during his mayoral year. He had worn it only once, 'cos their Mam had said it was common, so into mothballs it had gone, and emerged with the same ancestral smell as Amy's trousers.

'A bit of sea air will take the smell away,' Stan said, for he had to say something, since no verdict on his headgear was forthcoming from either of them.

'You've gone and hidden your lovely curls,' Gwyneth declared at last.

'I won't wear it then,' he said, throwing it on the table.

'You put it on your head, Stan,' Amy said quickly. 'Looks lovely, it does.' She wanted him to wear it. In a way it sanctioned their own fancy dress, hidden still behind the kitchen table.

'Come on then,' Stan said, 'or the sun'll go down.'

The picnic basket was ready packed, and there was nothing to keep the two women behind the counter. Amy made a quick calculation. If Gwyneth showed herself first, she would set the standard for Stan's trouser-judgement. And against Gwyneth's plump rigging, she swelled like a black and billowing sail. It was in her own interest to be the first on the cat-walk. She sidled around the table, keeping her broad beam to the wall, and presented Stan with a bold full frontal.

'Duw,' he said, and then again, 'Duw.'

'Don't want to wear anything too posh for the beach,' she almost apologised, absolving him from judgement. Nevertheless, he gave it.

'There's lovely you look, Amy,' he said. 'Slim like. You suit them, you do, don't they, Gwyneth? What about you then, girl? Look good on you too, they would.'

'See for yourself, then,' Gwyneth said, bold now, and walking the plank. And not just walking, but modelling too, back, front, and sideways, confident now that if in Stan's judgement Amy looked lovely, she, Gwyneth Price, was a veritable knock-out.

'Duw,' he said, and 'Duw,' again. 'The belles of Porthcawl you are, both of you. Women's liberation, that's what it is,' he said. 'Never thought we'd see it in our house though. Duw.' He was totally overwhelmed. He looked from one pair of trousers to the other, without any sense of comparison. That was a finesse that might or might not come later. At present he was engrossed in his outsize ladies' small revolution. 'Come on,' he said. 'Take me to the beach so's I can show you off.'

Amy put the hamper in his lap and Gwyneth wheeled him out of the house. Then Amy took over. 'My turn now,' she said, as if they were two children fighting over a doll's pram. Gwyneth obediently handed the steering over and Amy manoeuvred the chair to the cliff edge. 'We'll leave the chair here,' she said. 'Lock it I will. We can take him down that sand dune there.

It's not steep. There's a bit of sand by the bottom we can sit on.'

Gwyneth took his legs and Amy reached under his arm-pits. She had the heavier load, and having heaved him out of his chair she was forced to rest him on the sand to get her breath back. He lay helplessly on the slope. They were all breathing heavily, Gwyneth with most volume and least reason.

'You can wrap the blanket round my bum,' Stan said with a laugh, 'and shove me down the slope. No need to carry,' he said.

His idea was a practical one, but both Gwyneth and Amy wavered. Gwyneth was possibly wary of physical contact with Stan, especially around what she would have called his private parts, and therefore disgusting, but Amy was loathe to subject Stan to what she could only see as humiliating. To wrap a blanket round her brother's bottom was like putting a napkin on a baby, and Stan would surely feel it that way and be ashamed.

'We'll carry you,' Amy said. 'It's no trouble.'

But Stan had already taken the blanket, and managed, with much manoeuvring, to put it under one side of him. Amy rolled him over slightly, while Gwyneth, relieved of his body contact, drew the blanket underneath. Stan was able to hold it close in front of him. He was ready to slide.

Amy stood behind him and gave him a gentle push. There was no movement. Gwyneth took matters in hand. She stationed herself in front of him, crouching, and pulled him by the feet. What engine he had left to him kicked violently; he slid like a skate down the dune, knocking Gwyneth to one side, so that she too rolled down the slope, though with far less dignity. She landed on her elbows, having stuck them out to save the seat of the trousers made in Paris, France. But too late. The foreign material was no match for honest Welsh sand-grit, and the seat of her pants was frayed to a frazzle. Instinctively she clasped her hand to one side of her bottom, but in the few seconds that passed before she could clamp down on the other side, both Stan and Amy saw with their own eyes the blistered and trellised evidence of Gwyneth's secret.

Gwyneth Intacta Price wasn't wearing any knickers.

'Seen your bum, I did,' Stan shouted, which did not improve matters for poor Gwyneth, who felt they could now logically expect her to put her body up for sale.

'Your red bum,' Stan was shouting. His predilection for the word fed on its constant use. With each utterance, he stained it a little more, relishing its filth like a child. Gwyneth stood up, scratching in her mind for something that would explain her bloomer-less state. 'Could have sworn I put them on,' she said, her voice limping with the fraility of her excuse. But she could offer nothing else, nothing else that is that would not reflect on the quality and quantity of her lingerie. But that was not relevant either. The truth of her knicker-less state was not for the telling, for she could hardly admit it to herself. But if it were to be known, and put into words filth-proof enough to silence them, it was that the rub of serge on her bare loins was lovely, it was, and no one need ever find out, and what harm was there, she asked herself, if for the rest of her trousered life she could eavesdrop on the sweet congress between flesh and serge. 'Give yourself something to live for,' she had said to herself that morning in the joy of her discovery. Untellable, such tales.

'What an oversight,' she stumbled on. 'Will be losing my head next,' Forgetfulness was innocent enough and excusable, and her watering eyes begged them both to accept it and leave it be.

'We'll spread the table-cloth here then, shall we?' Amy said, changing the subject if not her focus, and Stan, too, dwelt on the fretted flesh, till Gwyneth, hitting on the only solution, sat down firmly on her shame.

Amy could see that Gwyneth was now planted immoveable for the duration, so it was up to her to drag up the sand dune and bring down the hamper. Yet she hesitated. It was not that she resented the donkey work. But she was loathe to leave Gwyneth and Stan alone. She was sorry for her friend, and she did not trust Stan in her absence to spare poor Gwyneth's blushes, or flushes, as Amy knew they must be by now, though Gwyneth had never mentioned them. They were disgusting things and didn't happen to the likes of Gwyneth. 'I do feel a bit hot Amy,' she had once confided, unable to hide the pink glow that crept up her cockeral neck. Mid-winter it was, in Amy's kitchen, with the snow on the sill. 'It's because it's so stuffy in here,' she said. 'You really should open a window.' Poor Gwyneth.

'Now you behave yourself, our Stan,' Amy said, trudging up the dune. And though she knew that, in the duration of her absence, Stan could blow his word a thousand times, relishing it no less in repetition, in spite of this she hurried, for there must come a time, she thought, when Gwyneth's back would break, and Amy would return before the thousand and first 'bum' was loaded.

'Don't you go falling now,' Stan called after her. "Two bare bums is more than I could bear.'

She heard him laughing, but she didn't look back, anxious to accomplish her mission and get back to maintain some kind of order. She felt the cloth of her trousers. It seemed hard-wearing enough. Maybe Gwyneth had been landed with a reject, a 'bummer', as no doubt Stan would have called it. As soon as the subject could be broached out of Stan's hearing, she would offer to darn them, for even Gwyneth would admit that Amy was the best darner in Porthcawl. A special skill, darning, that had nothing to do with practice, a skill that relied on a need, not to make do and mend, but to restore to the natural order of things.

She reached for the hamper and pulled it down the slope towards her. She would have to carry it, for there was too much that was breakable inside. She reached out to lift it up, and was suddenly transfixed, terrified of the descent. Stan and Gwyneth were only a few yards away, but she could in no way bridge the gap. Her knees were melting and her ankles shivered. 'I can't,' she shouted down to them, wondering what had come over her, and knowing that it had nothing to do with the weight of the hamper or the slope of the dune. Perhaps it was because she had caught sight of Gwyneth's hand on Stan's knee, and she could find no immediate reason to account for it. It was not rubbing it, as if massage had been called for, it was not fingering its cloth for its quality, it just lay there, claiming ownership. It was irrelevant that Stan had no feeling in his legs, but he could *see* it there, for God's sake, and he was doing nothing to remove it, so that it could well have been there from his own invitation. 'I can't,' she practically screamed at them, and, under her breath, 'You take your dirty rotten hand off my Stan's knee, Gwyneth Price, you and your bare bum, you harlot.'

'Give us a hand,' she shouted.

Gwyneth shifted about, loath to rise. Her hand remained on Stan's knee as if glued there.

'Oh, bugger your bum,' Amy shouted.

She saw Stan take off his jacket and hand it to Gwyneth, and this act of chivalry made her tremble with a sense of impending loss. She suddenly and very badly wanted to relieve herself. She sat down on the sand and waited.

Now Gwyneth took her hand away, and put on Stan's jacket. 'Look daft, you do,' Amy said spitefully. 'Doesn't cover anything anyway.'

'Duw, what's the matter with you then, girl?' Gwyneth said, climbing the dune.

'What's the matter with our Stan's knee, then?' Amy said, for it was better out than pickling sour inside her.

'Duw,' Gwyneth said, and another flush. 'There's hot it is in this coat,' she said.

'It's not hot at all,' Amy said with the authentic ring of a meteorologist. 'You're in the change, Gwyneth Price,' she said. 'The change of life,' she shouted, a warning, she hoped, calculated to put a stop to any budding affair. 'Getting on you are.'

'Speak for yourself then, girl,' Gwyneth huffed and puffed up the slope, totally ignorant of what had prompted Amy's show of malice. 'What's come over you anyway?" she said, drawing level and reaching down for the hamper. 'Only my hand it was on Stan's knee.'

Brazen with it too, Amy thought, and wondered what further part of her body Stan's knee would be easel to. She let Gwyneth carry the hamper down on her own, while she trod carefully behind, squinting at Gwyneth's frayed rear. Sew them up, I will, she thought, over-stitch, quick like, and terrible. Not worthy of one of my darns, she isn't.

'I'll spread the cloth,' Gwyneth said, opening the hamper.

'Now you sit down, Amy, and rest yourself. It's quite a climb up that hill. Well,' she said, bending over, 'no point in hiding it. You've seen it all now.' And she took off Stan's coat and handed it over to Amy, acknowledging that Stan, and everything about his person, belonged to his poor ugly sister. 'Change of life indeed,' she muttered to herself. 'Disgusting.'

'How's our Stan, then?' Amy said, her property returned.

'It's lovely here, isn't it?' he said. 'Don't know why we don't do it more often.'

'There's the whole summer to come,' Amy said. 'We'll treat ourselves.'

'You too, Gwyneth,' Stan said, and Amy was silent, not knowing what gnawed at her. She comforted herself with the thought that tomorrow was her poste restante day. There would be a letter. And then there would be her reply and consultation of the family album, and Stan in his room close to her own, and him all to herself for ever. Poor Gwyneth.

'There's nice you've done it, Gwyneth,' Amy said, regretting her former meanness. 'Laid it lovely you have.'

'Where's the glasses then?' Gwyneth said.

'Duw, I forgot,' said Amy, glad that there was something Gwyneth could blame her for.

But Gwyneth did not take the advantage. 'We'll have to drink out of the bottle then, shan't we.'

Stan uncorked the sweet sherry—a man's job—while Gwyneth doled out the chicken and the bread and butter. Stan took the first swig at the bottle, and handed it to Gwyneth. Amy's heart fluttered at the pecking order, but she patiently waited her turn. Gwyneth took her share, and then, wiping the top with a serviette, she handed the bottle towards Amy. Stan interrupted its passage, taking another swig, and Amy had to snatch it from him for her share. A gull's-eye view would have been a picture of three revellers, whole and hearty, and that same gull might have wondered why a cripple's chair stood above them on the dune, and had Stan looked up he might have wondered, too, for a touch of sweet sherry levelled them all. Between them, and quickly, they finished the bottle. Each of Stan's knees was capped with his ladies' liver-pocked hands, and though he could feel nothing, it was good to see them lying there. Sometimes, when he was alone, he would bend forward on his chair, and lay his hands on the top of his feet. Slowly he would move them up along his legs, first his ankles, then travelling to his shins and knees. And all the while feeling nothing. He knew with exact precision at what point in his leg his nerve would begin to respond. Some one and three-quarter inches over the top wrinkle of his knee-cap, if it were bent, and in a small pin-point along that line, lay the site of his first response, the astonishing sudden pulse that quickened as his hand slid higher. He looked at the women's hands. From what he could gauge with his highly practised eye, both were within two or three inches of life, and he stared at the limp knuckles of each of their hands and willed them to exploration. But they lay there content, capable, soap-powder-raddled both of them, unambitious and respectable. For all he felt of them they could well have been lying on their own knees. Yet it was good to see them there, visible contracts for his silent counter-signature. He nodded to show them both that it was good. They clenched their fingers over the bone. He thought of Blodwen, and how he would write and tell her about the picnic. To-morrow she would receive his latest missive. He wondered whether perhaps he'd gone too far. Slowly over the months he had tested her threshold, and she had responded without scruple. In fact, she herself had teased him to even greater heights. He thought perhaps that flesh proscribed its own limits, but that the horizon of words was infinite. He almost recoiled at the thought of ever seeing Blodwen face to face. Lately in his letters he insisted less on that possibility. What was left to do with a woman whose flesh one had minutely clothed in language, whose body one had conquered with idiom, whose appetite had been tamed with tongue. Yet had she been there on the beach, he would have freely taken her hand and placed it higher on his thigh. Gwyneth and Amy would have thought such a gesture disgusting. So he contented himself by just looking at their affection. He would tell Blodwen about them, and make her jealous.

Gwyneth cleared the lunch. She had to manage it sitting down, no longer because of her ventilated rear, but that the drink had unpinned her balance. Amy was already lying down, longing with every sweet-sherried part of her to sleep, but she did not trust Gwyneth with Stan.

'Leave it, Gwyneth,' she said. 'Have a little sleep now.' And Gwyneth would gladly have done just that, but that it meant doing Amy a favour, and though her lids drooped, she manfully stretched across the sand to gather the remnants of the lunch.

'Do what she says,' Stan said. 'We'll all have a little nap.' He eased his back down on to the sand, sanctioning them both to siesta. There was now no point in holding the fort, and Gwyneth slouched on the sand and fell asleep almost immediately. Amy was glad that Gwyneth was snoring, so that Stan could hear it loud and clear. Now it didn't matter if she snored too. Gwyneth wouldn't hear her, and sisters were anyway forgiveable. Stan listened to them with affection. 'They're growing old,' he thought, 'both of them.' And though he could have given them each a few years, he was younger than them by far. And his pram was on the top of the sand dune to prove it.

* * *

Coughing he was. Coughing something terrible. That silly bitch Gwyneth, Amy thought, insisting on wearing Stan's coat all the way back from the sands, and Stan shivering in his chair saying he didn't feel cold or anything. Her and her stupid bare bum. She couldn't leave him coughing like that, and his letter lying in the cubby-hole in Porth, singeing the wood with its ardour. The others would miss her too, that supercilious clerk at the counter and all the Thursday regulars. They might even think that her friend had found a house to her satisfaction, and they would write her off their list and show surprise if she ever turned up again. She cursed Gwyneth for interfering with her routine, and as she did so she saw her coming up the path, Stan's coat over her arm. She rushed to the door, not wanting Stan to hear the bell, but Gwyneth beat her to it, and three minims were out before Amy reached the door.

'He's coughing terrible,' Amy said, before Gwyneth had a chance to come in. She was laying the blame where it was due.

'Shouldn't have taken his coat,' Gwyneth said. 'It's been on my mind all night. Stan of all people can't afford it on his chest. Poor thing. Shall I sit with him a bit then, Amy?' she said. 'D'you want to go shopping?'

She seemed eager, too eager for Amy's comfort. 'It can wait,' Amy said, 'I'll do it tomorrow.'

'No, go on now, girl. I'll sit in the kitchen in case he calls.'

Amy was tempted. 'I've brought my trousers too,'

133

Gwyneth was saying. 'I'll have plenty to do while you're gone.'

'Got to go to Porth,' Amy said. 'Left my watch for mending.'

'Well then get going, girl, or you'll miss the bus. On the hour it is now.'

Once she'd reached the Post Office Amy felt safe. Having negotiated the streets of Porth without shameful encounter, she now felt herself amongst friends. It had become a regular and social occasion. Amy knew most of the clients, and those newly-recruited already looked upon her as an old-timer.

'Your friend not suited yet, Miss Pugh?' Mrs Williams said. Nobody in the Post Office believed that story, but they accepted it as a client's rightful camouflage.

'She's a bit fussy,' Amy said. 'Hard to suit. And the prices. Duw, they're rising terrible.'

She took her place in the line behind Mrs Williams. 'How's your Margaret, then?' Amy asked.

Mrs Williams beamed. Then, looking stealthily around her, she whispered into Amy's cheek. 'She's carrying.'

'Oh there's lovely,' Amy said. 'Perhaps he'll soften with a grandchild.'

'I'm hoping,' Mrs Williams said with little hope. 'Stubborn he is, my Emrys.'

The line moved forward as Mr Davies collected his Dai's letter. The clerk noted that Dai's communication lines were improving, and he said as much to Mr Davies.

'Only writes when he wants something,' Mr Davies mumbled.

'Got to count your blessings though,' the clerk said, his fingers running down the cubby-holes for his next client. She was the sad and demented war-widow, whose visits were the most regular and the most futile.

'Mrs Thomas,' she kept mumbling at the grille. '*Mrs* Thomas,' she said, stressing the prefix that she had happily savoured for a mere three weeks before her man's last letter had come. The clerk's finger trembled. He turned his back to the grille. 'Jesus,' he whispered. 'Good God mun, would you believe.' His knees were shaking but he managed to walk to the inner office to report the extraordinary turn to the sub-Post Master.

'What's the matter, Evans bach?' the manager said. 'White as a sheet you are.'

'Mr Jones,' the clerk squeaked, 'there's a letter for Mrs Thomas. Mrs Ruth Thomas. Plain as a bloody pikestaff in the cubby-hole. What am I to do then?'

'Give it to her, mun,' Mr Jones said, 'and God help her. There's some terrible tricksters around. Wouldn't think twice before doing the dirty. But then, it might be genuine. It just might, you never know. Either way,' he said, with an intuition born of a lifetime spent in communications, 'either way, poor soul, God help her.'

When Evans left his room, Mr Jones got up and went to stand at the glass door of his office so he could witness the transaction. Evans went back to the cubby-hole. He would have been relieved and unsurprised if the letter was not there after all, that it had been some desperate wishful thinking on his simple part, who, every week, for so many years, had witnessed the poor woman's despair. But it lay there as he had left it. Mrs Ruth Thomas. Dutch stamped and postmarked Rotterdam.

The delay caused by Evans' hesitation sent a ripple of rumour down the line. Already there was no doubt that a letter had arrived, and now there was speculation not only as to what it might contain but as to how the poor lady would receive it. The gentleman waiting in line behind her, himself a regular of many years standing, who was au courant with everybody else's secrets, but jealously guarded his own, now stretched his arm out behind the lady in expectation of her fall. A silence almost screamed in the Post Office. Any other business was put to one side, as all the clerks gaped in the direction of the war-maybe-not-widow. Evans turned from the cubby-hole, the letter burning his hand. He heartily wished he were not the carrier. What could he say to her as he handed the letter over? He was never at a loss for words of sympathy or celebration. But now only silence could cover his gesture, and he slipped the letter under the grille without even daring to look at her. But Mr Jones, by his glass partition, had a clean eye-full, and later in the day, and during the course of the next few weeks, for it was not a story that could lose by constant repetition, it was Mr Jones' testimony that found the hard core. All the others, the clerks at the adjacent counters, the regular clients, contributed each one to the story. But all of them lied like eye-witnesses. Mr Jones' deposition, from his glass-partitioned neutrality, was the most reliable. And this, over the next few weeks, with very little variation— proof of its authenticity—was how he told it.

'I told Evans, give it to her, I said, but God knows, I wasn't unmindful of the consequences. I didn't expect trouble, like, but I thought a little help might be needed, so I watched from the partition, where I'm standing now like, and you can see, all of you, it's a good vantage point to Evans' grille.'

At this point, he would stop in his narration, inviting any of those who needed proof of his reliability to come and test it for himself. Nobody did, of course, 'cos Mr

Jones was the boss-man, and it didn't do to question his honesty.

'I watched Evans hand the letter over—I was a bit sorry for him like—it's terrible being the bearer of bad news, and bad news I knew it was, and I'll tell you for why later.' Mr Jones had bardic potentials and he was keeping them in reverse. He paused while he put his quarry by. 'Well, Evans shoved the letter under the grille, gentle like, and the poor woman looked up at him. She opened her mouth for to speak like, and all I heard was a squeak. Then she staggered a bit, or so it looked from the half of her I could see, and Mr Rhys, who was standing behind her, caught her like, on his arm. She didn't faint exactly. Overcome she was. She picked the letter up, and there and then she started to cry. You couldn't hear her, it was silent like, but duw, you could see it on her face. Burning and soaked her cheeks were. "Shall I open it for you?" Mr Rhys said, and he wasn't prying or anything. He just thought it would help. And I'm sure the rest of the queue was glad of it. Curious they were, see. It's understandable like. For not every day in Porth Post Office does one get a letter after thirty-odd years. She looked at the envelope first. Typed it was, and important looking. Then she gave it to Mr Rhys. "Look out for the stamps now," she said, as if that was all she cared about. And probably it was,' Mr Jones said, drawing on his reserve, 'for she was afraid to face the important issue in hand. So Mr Rhys opened it, very careful like. "Mind the stamps," she said again. Well Mr Rhys handled that envelope like it was a new-born baby, and when it was open he took the letter out from inside. One page it was, folded. Nice and tidy. I could see it from where I stood. She held it for a bit, weighing it like, testing the matter of the words inside. Lightweight, she must have thought, because she handed it back to Mr Rhys like it was his problem. So he opened the fold. Mrs Thomas was right. It weighed nothing. Not a single word, neither front nor back. Blank it was, empty as a fart. I thought to myself then, there are some small-minded souls in this world, who'd trouble to do a disgusting thing like that. Even to the extent of going to the Netherlands to do it, or sending someone perhaps. And if I'd caught him ever, on my mother's grave I swear I would have killed him. And so did everyone else in the place, I'm sure. Except for Mrs Thomas. That was the strange thing. She laughed, d'you see. Not hysterical like, but smiling and happy. Now when I think of it, I understand why. I told you in the beginning that one way or the other the letter was bad news. Now I'll tell you for why. For thirty-odd years, Mrs Thomas has grown accustomed to an absence, she has grown accustomed to faith. Her lover is not Mr Thomas any more. Her lover is hope. With hope she beds each night; she greets each morning with sanguine expectation. She is affianced to a dream.' Mr Jones drew on his reserves in full. It was as if he were delivering an acceptance speech at the Eisteddfod, acknowledging the award of the bardic crown. Indeed, even the chair he sat on during his narration, took on the semblance of a throne. 'For thirty years, this fools' paradise has been her companion, her night and day co-traveller, confirmed every Thursday at our little counter. For a terrible moment when that letter came, she saw that dream shattered, and the long and empty days ahead. Twice in a lifetime widowed, bereaved by man and mist. No, my friends, God was good that day. It was no wonder she was joyful, my friends, for quietus is only the penultimate disclaimer. The final rejection is death of the imagination.'

Lifting the bardic crown, Mr Jones wiped his brow. It was a gesture he made after each performance. He'd made the tale so much his own, that other witnesses forbore to tell it. 'Ask Mr Jones,' they'd say. 'Tells it like a poet, he does.'

But Amy wouldn't tell it, like a poet or otherwise, though she itched to give Stan the story. But what was she doing in poste restante he'd want to know, and where else could such an incident have taken place? So she had to hold her tongue, though on the bus home she thought of it long and intensely, as Stan's latest hot missive cooled in her bag.

When she got home she saw Dr Rhys' car parked in front of the house. Stan had taken a turn in her absence. Gwyneth hovered guiltily in the kitchen.

'It's his chest, it is,' Amy said. 'Not surprising,' and she went straight to Stan's room.

'Bit of a chill he has,' Dr Rhys said. 'I've left some medicine. Should take care of that chest of his, you know.' Dr Rhys directed at Amy, as if Stan's chest were her own. Better tell that to Gwyneth, Amy thought. She looked at Stan's fevered face. 'Can't I go out at all?' he pleaded.

'What's so urgent that you want to go out for?' Dr Rhys asked. It was a letter to post, Amy knew, and it was to wheel his chair down to the bottom of the garden for the privacy of reading of Blodwen's love. She would reply to his letter tonight, Amy decided. As soon as she could get rid of Gwyneth. Cheer him up a bit, it would.

Dr Rhys left muttering, as if Amy needed any reminder of her brother's mortality. 'I know, I know,' she shouted at him.

'There, there,' he said, his arm on hers, 'but keep his chest covered. It's not summer yet,' he said. 'Said something about a picnic on the sands. That's where he caught it, no doubt. Keep the picnics for August, Amy. Sensible like.'

She wanted to kill him for his lack of feeling. No notion of other people's feelings, she thought. 'Well you'll go before my Stan,' she whispered under her breath, 'and it'll be your meanness'll carry you off.'

He left her in silence, so she stormed into the kitchen to vent her rage on Gwyneth.

'Ever so sorry I am,' Gwyneth said, before Amy could open her spluttering mouth. 'All my fault it is. Stupid that I am.'

She had said it all, and Amy sat silently. 'Take a week, the doctor said,' she said at last, 'and he'll be better. Thank you, Gwyneth, for sitting. I'm all right on my own now.'

Gwyneth was glad to leave. 'Say goodbye to him then,' she said. 'I'll be in with the bread in the morning.'

Amy started on her letter right away. She was worried about Stan, anxious that the post would catch him. So acute was her haste that she was well into the letter before she realised she had not thought about her style. She wrote nothing about her body, a subject that usually filled the first paragraph of every letter to Stan. Now fleshly digression seemed inappropriate. She was writing to Stan about poor Mrs Thomas. It was *her* pain that was more fitting for correspondence. Amy had been much disturbed by the incident. Mrs Thomas' story had been a painful confirmation of the way of life she herself was pursuing. She too was wedded to a fantasy, and it was unnerving to have a glimpse of fantasy-threat and to have an inkling of what disaster could ensue. She thought that if she wrote it down, if she could share it, especially with one who played a major, nay, the only role in her dream, it would secure the tenuous thread that linked them, on her side at least, where it was most fragile. For a long time she pondered as to where to locate the story, and finally decided that it had happened at the home of Blodwen's mother's friend, and that the tale had been told by Blodwen's mother. Instead of the intimidating Post Office cubby-hole, it became a threat that lay in a private letterbox. The matter and the message of the story remained intact. All it lost was its public humiliation, and Amy thought, as she wrote it down, that it lost little by that. Indeed, in private, the fear of it was greater, despair echoing in the empty hall.

When the story was told, unfolded in purple ink all over the page, it sprawled into a distance, disjoining Amy from its sinister overtones. Now her feelings for Mrs Thomas were solely of detached pity. It was nothing whatsoever to do with her. Thus relieved, she was able to devote the rest of her letter to satisfy Stan's fleshly appetites, and it had to be admitted, her own. In her P.S. she looked forward again to meeting him. 'My Mam's getting better,' she said. As she wrote of her Mam's progress, she heard Stan's raucous coughing from his room. 'Duw', she thought, 'my Mam'll be well, and I'll be able to get out, and Stan'll be ill, and confined to his house.' So she added to her letter, 'It seems we're destined not to meet, you and I, my lovely. P.P.S. In your next letter, tell me if you have any scars. I have, so there, but you must tell me about yours first. I bet you've got some like, 'cos duw, we've got so much in common.'

He was coughing still. Well, she thought, I shall have to leave my Mam one day, and pop over to Porthcawl to see him. Surprise him I will. She put the letter in the envelope. Mrs Thomas and her menacing story had drifted many miles away.

* * *

He coughed non-stop for a fortnight. Gwyneth came every day. She made no offer to Stan-sit again. Her visits seemed to be solely to Amy, to whom she felt more directly indebted. 'Stupid I was to take his coat,' she said every morning with the bread. Until it got on Amy's nerves long after she had forgiven her.

When the coughing stopped he was too weak to get up. Every morning, Amy asked him if he'd like a little walk, for she missed his letters terribly. 'What about your stamp catalogue?' she asked timidly one morning. He brightened a little. 'I think I'll send off for it,' he said, 'if you bring me paper and envelope.'

She brought them quickly, and left him to his Blodwen. Later on, he called her and asked her to take it to the post. 'Sorry to be such trouble,' he said.

'I'll drop it in the box now,' she said. 'It'll catch the afternoon post.'

She went back into the kitchen with the letter. She was sorely tempted. Had she opened it there and then, it would have saved her a journey to Porth on the following day. But she didn't want to interfere with the niceties of the production. The poste restante in Porth was as much part of the affair as the letters themselves. Besides, to open the letter would have been like taking advantage of a blind man's visual ignorance. No. It could only bode harm. Quickly she put on her coat and rushed to the post box.

He was well enough to get up the following day and Amy had no hesitation in asking Gwyneth to stay with him while she went shopping. And when she returned from Porth, Stan's letter in her bag, Gwyneth and Stan were doing a jig-saw on the kitchen table. Gwyneth offered to withdraw as soon as Amy arrived. Rather too readily, Amy thought, and she presumed that her friend still felt too guilty to accept hospitality that she was not earning.

'Stay,' Amy said. 'Finish the puzzle. I've got a few things to do upstairs.'

She took the letter to her bedroom and opened it straightway. In the early days of the first letters she would hesitate before opening them, partly to prolong the excitement but mainly out of fear of what the letter contained. Some impossible demand perhaps, some off-putting sentiment, rejection even. Now she had no reason to fear the contents or to prolong the excitement. They were no longer strangers to each other. They were secure in each other's impediments.

'My lovely Blod,' she read. 'Received your last letter, and thanks for same. What a tragic story about poor Mrs Thomas. Mind you, Blod, you're right. People do learn to live with their dreams. No one wants them shattered like. Which reminds me, if you and me don't get together soon, you'll be a bit of a dream yourself, love. And so will I for you. So I've been thinking. It's a bit difficult in my condition for me to come over to Porth, and I'm wondering if you could leave your Mam one afternoon and come over to Porthcawl. Duw, my insides are melting when I think of it. I'm worried, d'you see, and I'll tell you for why. If we don't meet soon, there'll come a time, like with Mrs Thomas, when we won't want to see each other, because we have relished our correspondence for so long. It has become the whole purpose of our relationship. Now I don't know about you, Blod, but as for me, I'm ready to meet you any time. You'll just have to let me know when you can come. I'll have to tell Amy then. You see, Amy doesn't know about us, not that I want to keep it secret like, but you know how it is, if you live with someone so long and they look after you, they get sort of possessive. She may be a bit jealous like in the beginning, so I'll have to talk her round to it. I hope in your next letter you will let me know of your arrangements. I can't wait to see you, Blod.'

Amy put the letter down. She was not surprised at the turn the affair had taken. That was to be expected. But she had delayed any thought about how to deal with it. She would put him off for a while, with one excuse or another; he would either settle for the dream of her, or fret to see it realised. If the latter, he might even look elsewhere, his appetite sharpened. She shuddered at such a possibility. Postponement was the only way open to her.

'What a time we'll have together,' the letter continued. 'I'll be able to see for myself the flesh of you, though you can be sure, I know it intimately from your letters. What a peculiar request you make about scars, Blodwen. I, too, am very interested in scars, but I've never liked to talk to anyone about it. Seems sort of daft. So I'm glad it's your hobby too, and I'm happy to oblige you with information. To be honest, I haven't got very many. Three to be exact. One on my elbow where I fell on the rocks when I was little. Four stitches, Blod. Duw, it was deep. The second one is on my leg where they tried to operate. Eight stitches in that one, and purple it is. Always has been. The third one is the best but I can't tell you about it because it's on a rude part. Very rude, and purple too.'

Amy smiled. As far as she remembered, and from bathing and caring for him she knew her brother's body intimately, there was no third scar. Not at all. He obviously never intended to prove it to Blodwen. His level of fantasy was high enough already. With luck it would extend to Blodwen herself.

'Now I've told you about mine, it's your turn. Please, Blod, tell me where they are, and what they look like, and be honest now, 'cos I shall want to see them when you come. Like I'll show you mine, except the third one, 'cos like I said before, it's rude. Oh, Blod, I forgot to tell you about our picnic. Three of us we were, myself, Amy and our friend Gwyneth. You would have laughed. My sister Amy, who, as I've told you, is a bit staid like, well she suddenly appeared in a pair of trousers. Looked lovely she did. Bit of a shock it was, specially when I saw Gwyneth was wearing them too. They're both a bit fat, mind you, but I like a bit of flesh on them. Duw, Blodwen, I got so excited at the sight of them, and so hot inside, that, if you will excuse me, I thought all day about you. You know what I mean, Blod, without speaking it out. Well, off we went down to the beach, and Gwyneth tripped and rolled down the dune, and in doing so, she split her trousers and Amy and me could see her bum. Her bare bum, Blodwen, 'cos she wasn't wearing any knickers. Disgusting I suppose, but nice it was, and I was sitting there on the sands, all hot inside me and—well you know what I mean, Blod—just thinking of you all the time. It makes me all trembly when I write about it. Look now, Blod, we've got to meet. In your next letter will you make some arrangements like, or I shall begin to feel like poor Mrs Thomas. Duw, I love you, Blod. Hoping this finds you as it leaves me at present. Yours, Stan.'

Amy smiled at the sudden intrusion of formality. She was aware though that something was missing, some piece of the normal pattern of communication had been lost. There was no P.S. For some reason it worried her. Stan's P.S.'s, like her own, were not after-thoughts. They were an integral part of the letter, and only appended because they were so super-charged, that their presence in the letter itself would have resulted in an explosion. So they had to be carried carefully and separately. She read the last part of the letter again. 'I love you, Blod,' he had written. He had meant it, she was sure, as a P.S., but it had exploded prematurely, and his last formal phrase had been by way of clearing up the pieces. Yes, she thought, he did love her, whoever 'her' was, but what did it matter if the target were a fantasy. His quiver was full and his aim was sure.

She added the letter to her collection, and re-tied the red ribbon. She was very careful with the bow, straightening it at the edges. Though the pile was thick and solid now, she held it with infinite care, for she knew its cardinal fragility.

She shivered with the excitement of Stan's declaration, and she wanted somehow to celebrate it. As she put the letters in her drawer she noticed an old lipstick that had once belonged to her mother. Never in her life had she used cosmetics of any kind. There was no cream in the world to unstub her nose, or contract her pier-like chin. She had accepted the fact that her ugliness was beyond mending, that one might as well apply maquillage to a gargoyle. But now, as she looked at herself in the mirror, she saw herself as a love-object. Gently she fingered the contours of her face, and for the first time in her life she would not have changed it for any other. Tenderly she painted her lips with her Mam's leavings.

She walked boldly into the kitchen. Gwyneth and Stan were still at the jig-saw, and neither looked up when she entered. She had been prepared for their immediate verdict, and now that she had to hang around and wait it made her nervous and she was tempted to go back and wipe it all away.

'Like my lipstick, then?' she said, bold as brass, more comfortable to draw attention to herself.

They looked up. 'Dis—,' Gwyneth started.

Had Stan been mobile he would have rocketed out of his chair, for all his body was soaring. 'Duw,' he said, and it was all he could get out, for he salivated from both corners of his mouth.

Gwyneth looked at him, astonished. The interest now lay more in Stan's reaction than in what had triggered it off. She thrust her chest out at him, availing herself of the tease that she knew was inevitable, as part of his expression of surprise, and he promptly pinched her under her left breast to seal his amazement. 'Duw,' he said again.

'You've got lipstick on,' Gwyneth said, because somebody had to say something. 'Give us a bit then.'

Though there was not as yet a specific role for Gwyneth she joined the cast automatically. The make-up department had to be open to her too. Amy felt no resentment. Apart from the occasional scratch of irritation, her feelings towards Gwyneth were of pity. She pitied her for having no pen pal, for having no reason on earth to expect the future to be anything more exciting than a prolongation of the dreary present.

'Up on the dressing-table,' she said, as an act of kindness. 'Suit you it will.'

But when Gwyneth came downstairs again, her lips red-slashed, Amy was suddenly uneasy, as she watched Stan, drooling with joy over his eye-full of promising cherry.

* * *

Amy waited for a while before she replied to Stan's letter and his request for a visit. She hoped for a cooling-off period. She knew that she could prevaricate a little longer, but there would come a time when Stan would demand to be satisfied. There was nothing she could do about that, and when that time came the correspondence would have to cease, so Amy dared not think about such a time. A Porth-less, letterless future was unbearable. So, as she wrote, postponing her visit, she increased her verbal ardour not realising that her words could only feed Stan's frustration. For on receipt of the letter postponing her visit he fell into a sullen mood. He began to find fault with Amy's care for him. His erstwhile gratitude that she had once found so irritating had turned to gloom. More and more he asked for Gwyneth but not for company or friendship, but simply as another target for his hostility. And Gwyneth obliged. 'It's the change of life,' she whispered knowingly to Amy. 'Men get it too. And little wonder with him sitting there all his life, with all his feelings stifled like, not getting the air.' She was full of knowledge was Gwyneth, and Amy let her rattle on. As so often, Gwyneth was partly right, but wholly for the wrong reasons. Amy was at a loss how to handle this unexpected turn of events. So she postponed thinking about it. She would wait for his next letter.

But he kept her waiting. For the first time in her Porth excursions, her cubby-hole was empty. The clerk tittered his sympathies, and he hoped that she would come again. 'You never know—the post nowadays, Miss Pugh, unreliable. You'll be in next week now, won't you?' Mrs Williams, too, was sympathetic. None of them wanted to see a regular fall away. There was a security every week in seeing the same faces. It was a threat if a regular left. For once you lost the need for your own cover, that of the other clients became less precious, and could be bandied around to all and sundry. 'See you next week,' Mrs Williams almost ordered. 'There'll be two for you by then.'

On the bus on the way home Amy was forced to entertain the thought that the correspondence had come to an end. She sought in her mind for means to revive it, for promises that need never be fulfilled. She decided that she would write to Stan immediately, swallowing her pride, exulting him in her flesh and his, and try to rekindle the fires that once had burned with such ferocity.

He was in his room when she got home, and he didn't call out when her key turned in the door. 'Stan,' she called.

'I'm here,' he shouted. 'Where d'you think I could be, then?'

She didn't go to his room. She went straight to her own and started on her letter. She had no problem in dealing with her pride. What worried her was a terrible gnawing guilt that, by her own painful efforts, she had awakened in Stan such hope, such a life-appetite. It would have been better had he never felt at all, had he remained cooped in his chair and his terrible gratitude, sweating with his martyred sweetness. She had sprouted him, and left him dry. So she would give him no more flesh in her letter. She would ask his forgiveness.

But for what? To what sin could she plead guilty without revealing the entire deception. She could not diminish him so. But she needed forgiveness. For her own sake she had to beg his pardon. 'Stan beloved,' she wrote. 'Forgive your teasing Blod. Duw, I would love to see you, too. But my Mam, bless her soul, has taken a very bad turn. Old age, the doctor says. Tired, she is. Don't leave her Blodwen, he says to me. She can go any time. So you see, my beloved, even to go out and post a letter to you is a risk, but I cannot bear not to write to you. Letters are a great solace.'

She put the pen down. She was hopeful. Stan could hardly expect priority over a moribund old lady. And as long as Amy kept her dying, she could always give Stan hope for her final release. For the meeting that could take place without impediment. Her Mam could decently and stubbornly take months over dying, and then would come another reprieve, the period of mourning which Stan would respect and perhaps even admire. And then the problem would again demand solution. She realised that Death was both her enemy and friend. As a friend, it would first claim Stan, taking him in the full bloom of his love, ignorant of the lies she had woven. As an enemy, it would call first on her Mam. There and then, she decided on her Mam's immortality. It was not that she was sentencing Stan. She was but adding mileage to the race.

'I was a bit worried like,' she wrote on, 'not having a letter from you this week. After all these weeks of going to the Post Office, the disappointment was terrible. I do hope now that you were not upset with my last letter, and I know you will believe me when I say that one day we will meet, and then this terrible waiting will be over. Oh, I do want to see you Stan. Love from my heart, Blodwen. P.S. I send my caresses to your third scar.'

She read it over and was satisfied. But as she wrote her home address on the envelope, she realised how the deception had engulfed her too. She was amused how one part of her could believe in it totally. She had to hold on firmly to the reason why she had started it in the first place. It was to give Stan something to live for. At the time she had not realised how deeply she herself would be involved. Now perhaps she stood to lose more than Stan.

She fingered the locket on her neck. Together with the pile of red-ribboned letters, it spelt out the only love she had known in all her sixty-odd years. Whatever happened in the future, it could not now be taken away from her. She tried to count the blessings of that, over and over again, but it seemed a kind of abdication. 'He *will* write to his Blodwen again,' she whispered, and for the first time in many months, she found herself crying.

* * *

She waited patiently till the following Thursday. Since his receipt of her last letter, she had watched him very closely. His temper had not improved. Even Gwyneth found the going rough. She still brought the daily bread, but Amy always had to persuade her to stay for breakfast. He was silent most of the time, spending the better part of the day in his room.

'It's the change,' Gwyneth would whisper every morning when she left. 'Happens to men—'

'You keep saying that, girl,' Amy interrupted her. 'But it's more than that,' she confided. 'It's losing his will, he is.'

'Rubbish,' Gwyneth shouted, 'you mark my words, girl, he'll outlive us all.'

On Thursday she left the house early, but she dawdled from the bus stop. She feared yet another disappointment. If the cubby-hole were empty she felt she would be letting Mrs Williams down too, and all the regulars who hoped weekly for each other's satisfaction. She forced herself to consider the possibility that he hadn't written, and the need to postpone such thoughts made her quicken her steps, and she had reached the Post Office before she dared entertain them.

She was early. Mrs Williams had not yet arrived and she found herself in a very short queue behind poor Mrs Thomas. She prayed that Mrs Thomas' hole would be empty, as the sad lady would wish, and that it would be a good omen for herself. Mrs Thomas reached the grille, waited for the formalities to be over, gladly accepted the clerk's negative, and went away happily empty handed.

'Pugh,' Amy said, reaching the grille. The clerk turned to the holes. Over his shoulder Amy could see the 'P' hole, and it was surely tenanted. She held her breath for Blodwen. The clerk extracted a letter.

'So glad you're not disappointed again, Miss Pugh. Thought we might have lost you.'

She gave him a smile for the first time, relief welling in her heart. As she left the Post Office, Mrs Williams was arriving. 'Lucky you are, then?' she said.

Amy smiled. 'I'm so glad,' Mrs Williams said. 'Thought we might be losing you.'

'I'll be coming in any case,' Amy heard herself saying.

'Now you mustn't go and get yourself like Mrs Thomas, dear.' Mrs Williams tried to put it gently. She, like the others in the line, had long since ceased to believe in Amy's house-buying story, for from Amy's Thursdays demeanour it was clear that such anxiety could not be on account of real estate, and certainly not on behalf of a second party. Mrs Williams' remark, though meant kindly, had frightened Amy, and she longed to open Stan's letter to dispel her fears. But the production that she herself had engineered did not allow her to open it on the bus. She had to wait rest-

lessly at the bus stop, and clutch it away from temptation all the way home.

She had left Stan alone that morning. She had
anticipated Gwyneth's refusal to Stan-sit, so she had
not asked for her help. Stan had been happy to be left
alone, and he was irritated when Amy assured him
that she would not be away for long. She hurried home
from the bus stop, expecting no welcome, but grateful
for the privacy of her own room. Once there, she tore
the letter open. 'Blodwen my dearest,' she read, and her
heart leapt with hope. 'I was sad to hear that your
poor Mam had taken a turn, and I hope she will get
better soon. As to myself, I have been thinking a lot
about us. I didn't write last week 'cos I was in the
middle of thinking. And now I've come to a decision.
I'm not satisfied, d'you see, with letters. I have been
very moody these last weeks on account of my frustra-
tions. And it isn't fair to our Amy who does her best to
understand. So I have come to a decision. Either I see
you very soon, or we must stop this writing. Either way
it will pain my heart, but in the long run I assure you,
it will be better for me. It's a bit of an ultimatum, isn't
it, Blod? I don't want it to sound that way. But I must
see you soon, 'cos I am hot inside. You've stoked me,
you see Blod, and I hope I've been a stoker for you too.
Duw cariad, let's get together, for God's sake. Yours
hotly, Stan. P.S. I mean it, Blod. Come or it's the
end.'

She put the letter down, shaking. Her Mam's immortality was no longer feasible. She knew she had no
choice. This letter would be her last. She would not
reply. She would add it to her collection, and on the
ribboned bundle she would stamp a seal. She would
wear the locket still, and she would never go to Porth
again. She would accept Stan's sullenness which could

now only grow more acute, and she would begin again to hate him.

She touched her nose, seeking its stubby outline. Now it re-affirmed itself, together with her jutting chin. and the total ugliness that now homed in full cry beneath her hand. 'I can't go back to all that,' she thought. 'What am I to do with *my* full-grown appetite, for God's sake?' There had to be another way. Some believable way to persuade him that a meeting in the future were possible. Some contrivance that would enter into competition with, God forgive her, Stan's own death-shadow, a contrivance that only at the very last moment would cede the race.

It would take a bit of planning.

*　　*　　*

The following day, when Gwyneth came with the bread, she too decided that something had to be done. She missed the Stan of red-letter days. Over his sullenness her bruises had healed and left her hungry for more. She wanted the old Stan back again. She brought an extra large loaf of bread, and stayed without permission for breakfast.

'What about spending the day with me then, Stan?' she said. 'Our Huw's coming over this afternoon. I could take you back with me after breakfast.'

'Go on,' Amy said. 'Be a change for you. You've been a bit low lately.'

He did not look up from his food. 'Wouldn't mind spending the day in Porth,' he said to his plate.

'Porth?' said Gwyneth. 'Whatever for? Nothing to do in Porth.'

'Just like to walk round a bit,' he said to his eggs. 'Haven't been there for ages.'

'Walk round in Porth?' Gwyneth said. 'Duw, might as well take a walk round the cemetery.'

'It's Porth I want to go to,' he said stubbornly. He looked pleadingly at Amy. 'Would you take me there then?' he said.

'I'll take him,' Gwyneth said quickly. 'Just for the morning. Then we'll come back and see Huw. You can have the whole day Amy,' she said.

Stan was immediately grateful. It was obviously a matter of indifference to him who took him to Porth. Amy wondered what he intended to do there. Whether perhaps he might call in at the Post Office just to look at the cubby-hole for traces of his love. Or perhaps he would ask Gwyneth to wheel him down the High Street where he might recognise Blodwen shopping. She feared for the burning hope in his heart and the quiet let-down of his return. 'What'll you do there all morning?' she asked nervously. 'We'll find something, won't we, Gwyneth,' he said, and for the first time in weeks, he nudged her, and Gwyneth was gratefully back in business.

Stan took a long time dressing. Amy did not comment on the perfumed smell of him, or the fact that he was wearing his best suit. Gwyneth by some rare instinct held her peace, too, and proudly she wheeled him out of the door, Porth-ways.

Amy gave them time to have boarded the bus, and taking a photograph of Blodwen from the album she left the house for Cardiff. She knew simply where she was going, but she had no plans as to what to say when she got there. She hoped that something would come to her on the long bus ride, but she kept postponing it, and the bus was drawing into Cardiff station, and she still had no notion of her lines. She went to the nearest telephone kiosk and checked the directory for the address she required. She knew it was not far from the station. She set out to cover it on foot. She did not want to ask directions of anybody. There was no need for anyone to know her business, since she hardly knew it herself.

She wandered for half an hour before she found Motcomb Street, and then when she looked down one end of it she could see the bus station. But she was glad she had not asked. She was in no hurry to widen the net of deception which must result from her plan. She kept telling herself that a letter-less future was unbearable and that what she was about to do was for the salvation of both of them. She stopped outside No 23. She knew it was the right address, but nevertheless she read the plaque over and over again. 'Simmons. Actors Agency Ltd.' She looked around furtively before entering. Then when the street was clear, she hurried through the open door. She felt as if she were entering a brothel. She walked to the door marked 'Enquiries' and knocked timidly.

'It's open,' someone called from inside.

Amy pushed the door. The woman behind the desk looked up at her, assumed she was a new client, and wondered what part on earth the poor lady hoped to play. 'We're not taking on anyone new,' she said, while Amy was still at the door. 'Can't find enough work for the ones we've got.'

'I don't want a job,' Amy said proudly. 'It's me that's offering employment.'

The woman stood up. 'Won't you sit down?' she said.

'I'd like to see the person in charge,' Amy said. She had no story ready, but she certainly was not going to waste even an unprepared version on someone who was not in authority.

'I'm in charge here,' the woman said. 'My name is Mrs Simmons. Do sit down.'

Amy took the edge of the seat. She opened her bag and fingered Blodwen's picture.

'You are a casting director?' Mrs Simmons asked.

Amy shook her head. She was not sure what that profession was, but it certainly was not hers, nor did she represent anything that would be remotely concerned with the agency. 'I've got an unusual request,' Amy began. It didn't feel as if she were talking. It was as if she were dictating a letter and she would not have been surprised if Mrs Simmons had taken up her shorthand notebook. 'I don't know quite how to begin.'

'Is it an actor you want?'

'Well an actress really.'

'What production is it?'

'Well it's like this,' Amy began again, edging still further on her chair. 'I want a woman who resembles this lady.' She handed the photograph over. 'If you can help me, Mrs Simmons,' she said, 'I'll tell you after for why.'

Mrs Simmons looked at Blodwen. 'There's a Welsh face if ever I saw one,' she said. 'I can match that with little trouble. And so long as it is an acting job, I can help you.'

'Oh it's acting all right,' Amy said, 'and an act of charity as well.'

'We charge for each performance,' Mrs Simmons said, wanting to make it clear that hers was a professional business.

'Duw. I wasn't thinking anything else,' Amy said. She was beginning to feel more at ease. The nature of the reserves she was drawing on was in itself fraudulent. An actor's pursuit was one of professional deception. The difference between herself and whoever was to play the part of Blodwen was simply one of subsidy. 'It's like this, Mrs Simmons,' she said. 'What I'm going to say must be confidential. I take that for granted.'

Mrs Simmons nodded, a Judas-nod, Amy thought, but that was a risk she had to take. 'It's for my brother like, Stan. Stan Evans. He's a cripple and dying, he is.'

Mrs Simmons shook her head sadly. She could see the set clearly. An old man in his wheel-chair by the fireside, his spinster sister tucking in his blanket, and the doorbell about to ring with the first piece of plot.

'For the past few months,' Amy went on, 'he's had a pen pal. A lady in Porth by the name of Blodwen Pugh. That's her photograph. I haven't seen the letters, of course, but Stan tells me about her. Now I don't want your actress to let on that Stan tells me about Blodwen. It would be a breach of confidence.'

Mrs Simmons dropped a theatrical nod once again.

'Well, he's dying you see, like I said.' She clutched fiercely on her locket in an effort to ward off the evil eye, 'though he doesn't know it, I don't think, and his great wish is to see Blodwen in the flesh.'

Mrs Simmons was not given to literary interpretation, and this time, to Amy's relief, her nod was innocent. Amy had a fleeting sense of triumph in conning her.

'Why is it then,' Mrs Simmons said, 'that Blodwen can't see him?'

'Well, I'm coming to that,' Amy said, 'which is why I've come here, d'you see. Blodwen has an invalid mother and she can't leave her. I'm sure she can't be aware of our Stan's condition, or she would move heaven and earth to see him. She doesn't know the urgency, d'you see, and it's not for me to tell her. So I want to pretend that she can get away from the house once in a while and come and see our Stan. So it's an actress I need, Mrs Simmons, and a good one, too.'

'What exactly will she have to do?' Mrs Simmons said. 'I mean, what must she say?'

'Well,' Amy said, 'I would have to see her beforehand like, and tell her all she's supposed to know about him, and what he knows about her, through the letters you see. Just sit and talk to him like. Nothing more than that.'

'But afterwards,' Mrs Simmons said, 'he'll write to the real Blodwen and say it was nice to see you. What do you do about that?'

Amy hesitated. That had not been a problem for her, and she had not anticipated that Mrs Simmons would see it as an obstacle. 'Duw, I never thought of that,' Amy said. Then, suddenly inspired, 'I've got a solution. The actress will have to make Stan promise not to mention it in his letters, in case her Mam should read them, and then she'd know Blodwen had skipped off. She's got a terrible Mam,' Amy added as if this would strengthen her solution. 'In any case,' she whispered, 'he's not going to live long enough to send any more letters. Death's hard, Mrs Simmons,' she said, 'but there's no doubt about it, it solves certain problems.'

But Mrs Simmons still found loopholes in the arrangement, and rightly so, but she could find no way of overcoming the snags. 'I must protect my clients, Miss Evans, you see.'

'All right then,' Amy said, in order to satisfy her. 'I'll let him write what he likes, but I won't post them. That will solve everything. Then all the actress must do is visit him from time to time. It won't be for much longer, Mrs Simmons.'

'But what will the real Blodwen think when the

letters stop. She'll write, won't she. She'll want to know why he hasn't written.'

'I collect the post every morning,' Amy said. 'I won't give them to him.'

'It's all very complicated indeed,' Mrs Simmons said. 'I don't like it very much, though I'm sorry for your poor brother.'

'Please,' Amy said. She didn't feel like going to another agency and spreading her mess of a tale. 'He's dying,' she said.

'All right,' she said at last. 'I'll go along with you, as long as you play your part as you say, and as long as my client is willing.'

Amy beamed with gratitude. 'You are more kind than you know,' she said.

So they arranged the transaction. Amy was to meet the actress and put her in the details of the picture beforehand. It was accepted between them as a conspiracy, but since it was on behalf of a dying man it was considered respectable. It even merited a contract, which Amy had to sign on the dotted line. Mrs Simmons handed her the pen, and she started to sign 'Blodwen'. Quickly she crossed it out and as she wrote 'Amy Evans' she trembled like a forger.

*　　*　　*

Miss Blodwen Pugh, alias Miss Marion Morgan, was to come on a Sunday. Tea it was to be, and had been so arranged. Miss Morgan was to arrive at four o'clock. Amy would leave the tray in the kitchen and make herself scarce. She was satisfied with Mrs Simmons's choice. Miss Morgan looked uncommonly like Blodwen, and she learned her part with a natural skill. Amy had gone again to Cardiff to meet her, to introduce her to

Blodwen's family or those with whom Stan was familiar. Her brother was a quiet man, Amy told her, not given to much talking, so she would have to keep the conversation going her end. She could invent whatever stories she wished as long as she kept within the framework of a life spent in Porth, with summers at the sea. Miss Morgan was excited by the assignment. She'd never done anything like it before. She usually played the role of servant in domestic comedies, but it was her simple ambition to play St Joan. 'This'll be good practice for you,' Amy encouraged her, though you're too old and too fat and too Welsh, Amy thought. She was growing rather fond of Miss Morgan.

When she returned from Cardiff she wrote to Stan straight away. 'Duw Stan,' she wrote, 'I know blackmail when I see it. But I'm giving in to you, you wicked thing. I'll skip off on Sunday next and come to tea. Four o'clock, or roundabout, depending on the bus. I won't write any more at present. I'll just count the days till Sunday. Hoping you will do the same, Yours, Blod. P.S. Duw.' It was the most super-charged afterthought of their entire correspondence.

When the letter arrived, she watched hawk-like for his reaction. When he came in for breakfast he seemed stunned. 'What's the matter, then?' she said, since his pale face called for some comment.

'Nothing,' he said, and he smiled a little. When Gwyneth came with the bread he practically raped her. Gwyneth feigned disgust, but inside she trembled. Stan waited for Gwyneth to leave before he broached the subject with Amy. He shifted his chair round the kitchen table. Amy feigned indifference at the sink, and with her back to him, she practised a look of astonishment and pleasure.

'Amy,' he said. 'I've got something to tell you like.'

She kept her back to him as she thought he would have wished. 'Oh yes,' she said. 'What is it?'

'I've got a lady friend.'

She fixed her face and turned around. 'Go on,' she said, 'Tell me another one.'

' 'Sright,' he said. 'Her name's Blodwen Pugh.'

'But that's the stamp catalogue lady.'

Stan looked at her. 'Well she wasn't,' he said. 'Had to say something, didn't I? Didn't want to let on.'

'How d'you get to know her?' Amy said.

'Wrote to her I did. She had an advertisement in the paper.'

'Duw,' Amy said, 'why you telling me now then?'

'Oh Amy,' he said, his lips trembling. 'She's coming. She's coming this Sunday for tea.'

'Want me to meet her, then?' Amy turned back to the sink. A strange jealousy gnawed at her.

He didn't answer immediately. 'Well,' he started, 'just to let her in like. You see, Amy,' he went on, 'it's the first time I'll be seeing her, and well, you know, she won't have a lot of time, 'cos she's got to get back to her Mam in Porth, so if you'd go out like, I could have her all to myself.' He said it in one breath to get it over with, for he feared that Amy would be hurt by his suggestion.

'Then I'll make you both a nice tea, I shall, and leave it all laid in the kitchen. Now I don't mind at all Stan,' she added quickly, 'just so long as I can have a dekko like.'

He wheeled his chair towards her. 'What'll we have for tea then?' he said.

'A trifle of course. It's Sunday.' She decided that she would use only a small drop of sherry. That Miss Morgan lady was being paid enough.

Between then and Sunday Stan did not mention the

subject again. But by the end of the week Gwyneth was applying hot compresses to her gratefully bruised flesh. By Sunday Amy had lost her appetite for the whole conspiracy, and she prayed that Miss Morgan would drop dead on her way to the première, whatever the consequences.

Stan was up early, busying himself in his room. She wondered what he could be doing. Eaten with jealousy, she peeped through the keyhole, but he had taken the precaution of stuffing it, which only increased her nagging curiosity. She heard the rustle of many papers and she concluded that he was foraging underneath his mattress. She smiled. Poor Miss Morgan. She was in for a rough ride.

At lunchtime he emerged from his room, his ears glowing. He had on his best suit, with a silk cravat in place of a tie. He looked very handsome, and Amy told him so. 'What you going to wear for your wedding then?' she teased.

'I *shall*,' he said, 'if she's willing.'

'Giving me the push then, are you?' she said.

'You'll come and live with us Amy. Then we can look after *you*. Buy a house we will. Porthcawl I prefer, if she's willing.'

'What about her Mam?'

'She'll die soon,' Stan said, with the solid conviction of an immortal. He had everything planned in his mind, and Amy feared for him. 'You may not like her,' she said. 'Letters are one thing. Flesh and blood's another.'

'But I've got her photograph,' Stan said. 'I like the look of her. Want to see it?' He wheeled himself to his room before she could answer. 'She's got one of me, too,' he shouted from the hall.

Amy looked at the photograph. It looked more like

Miss Morgan than the copy she had taken to Cardiff. 'She's a warm-looking woman,' Amy said.

'Warm's the word,' said Stan, barely able to contain himself.

'Well the trifle's ready,' she said, 'and I've made you some nice salmon sandwiches. Want to make a good impression, don't we, Stan? I shall answer the door,' Amy said, full of organisation, 'and I shall tell her to wait in the parlour. Then I shall go out. When shall I come back Stan? How shall I know she's gone?'

'I'll stick the broom out of the kitchen window,' he said, 'when it's all clear. You'll be able to see it from the street. You don't mind now, do you Amy?' He wheeled his chair close. 'I'll do the same for you,' he said.

'That'll be the day,' Amy laughed. 'An old spinster like me.'

'Well I'm a cripple, and that's worse,' Stan said.

'S'easier for a man,' Amy said.

He left it at that. He had no proof of it being otherwise.

Shortly before four o'clock, he went to hide in his room.

'Wish me luck, Amy girl,' he said, as he closed the door on her.

'If I weren't your sister I'd marry you myself,' she said.

Amy went back to the kitchen and waited too. For the first time since she had conceived the plan, she realised the pitfalls of the arrangement. If the Morgan encounter turned sour, the lady might, despite all promises of confidence, decide to blow the gaff, and the resulting humiliation for Stan would be unbearable. When Miss Morgan came, she decided that once again she must press upon her the need for absolute confidence. Then she would leave them to each other.

At four o'clock the four long minims rang out in the hall. Miss Marion Morgan was nothing if not on cue. A strangled cry came from Stan's room.

'I heard it,' Amy said. She opened the door. Miss Morgan had dressed well for the part. In sober yet attractive grey, with a white hat. She carried a bunch of roses, an item, Amy was given to understand, that would be filed on the expense sheet under 'Props'.

'I'm Miss Pugh,' Miss Morgan said, loud enough for Stan's eavesdropping. 'I've come to see your Stan.'

'I'm Stan's sister,' Amy said, having learned her words, too. 'It's very nice to meet you. Will you come inside?' She ushered Miss Morgan quickly into the parlour, where once again she insisted that however the interview turned out, there must be no breach of faith. Miss Morgan promised once again. She was anxious to get on with it.

'I'll call my brother now,' Amy said loudly. 'I have to go out, I'm afraid, Miss Pugh, but I hope I shall see you another time. Stan?' she called. Then she went to her bedroom, her part over. She did not listen. But she could not help hearing Stan's wheel-chair in the hall, the closing of the parlour door, and then, shortly afterwards, the opening and closing of the door of his bedroom. She crept down the stairs. In the hall she hovered. There was no sound from Stan's room. Then she heard a sudden outbreak of giggling and she could not bear to listen any longer. She went quickly out of the house, slamming the front door behind her.

She walked aimlessly. She was unable to shift her thoughts from Stan's room. She wondered whether Miss Morgan was steering the conversation and, if so, in what direction. She did not know where to go. She would have to hang around until the broomstick beckoned her from the window. Miss Morgan was being paid by the hour, and it was up to her to assess when her part had run out. If she stayed for only a short while, Amy would be relieved, but a short visit would also indicate an element of failure. If she stayed for long, Amy would have to linger in nail-biting envy. Either way, Amy could not be satisfied.

She looked back along the road. Her kitchen window was still visible in the distance. It was broomless. She turned down towards the cliff and the path to the beach. She rarely went to the sands on a Sunday. She had inherited her mother's sense of propriety regarding Rest Bay, and like the benevolent owner of a stately home she allowed the weekends for those less fortunate. But she needed the beach today, as she had at those times in her childhood when her Mam's prison on the hill had become too painful. She had to escape before her violence confounded her, as it threatened to do now.

The picnic baskets were everywhere, and hurdles of deck-chairs, and fat pigeon-valley trippers. She made for the rocks. She had to climb quite far into the inlet of the sea before she could find some spot where she could be alone. And although she still knew the rocks by heart, her familiarity, because of her age, was now dangerous. So she forced herself to go slowly, and when she reached the flat resting-place she sat quietly and waited for the gulls. It was one of the rocks on which she had sat as a child, nibbling at her stick of rock, and listening to the birds' call. Slowly the magic returned, the sea-smell, the frothing waves breaking on the rocks below. The memory of the house on the hill was now less painful. Whoever was the recipient of Stan's love, it was she who had made that love available. It was she who had pointed out to him the promised land, which, no doubt, even at this moment, he was entering. She was the host to his present ecstasy, and there was some vicarious joy in that. Even so, she hoped that Miss Morgan was not going beyond the bounds of her contract. That was limited to conversation. For anything beyond that, Amy would dock the fee.

Time was passing, but Amy was in no hurry to return, even if the broomstick was screaming out of the kitchen window. It was peaceful on the rock, and safe with the gulls' occasional 'Cawl'. She considered that she was not unhappy; that unhappiness indeed was not a condition that could persist for ever. The permanent continuation of such a state had been the ever-present fear of her childhood, a fear that had pursued her throughout the years, finding an obliging warrant at every turn. Now she knew that unhappiness did not cease. It was simply a condition that one grew out of. Yes, she decided. She was content.

She sat there, waiting for the trippers to depart. She looked at the litter they had left, and felt no resentment. The gulls perched and took off, even though she still sat there and was looking at them. When she was a child she had trusted them never to leave her. Now gulls were not what they used to be, but by that token neither were her needs.

Sh climbed the cliff, and from time to time she looked back at the sea. The gulls were taking off, but she no longer saw it as rejection. For the first time she thought of her Mam without hate, and though she knew that never in memory time would she love her, she could already think of her with pity.

From the top of the cliff she saw the broomstick of the All Clear. She did not hurry. She didn't particularly want to know how Stan had spent his afternoon. She simply wanted assurance that Miss Morgan had kept her promise, and that was quickly given by the look on Stan's face as he came into the hall to meet her. He glowed. Childlike beads of sweat stood on his forehead, as if he'd run all the way from an exploding secret, his heart pumping with its discovery.

'Was it nice then?' Amy said.

'Oh Amy,' was all he could manage.

He wheeled himself after her into the kitchen. The tea-tray lay untouched on the table, the cream-topped trifle still whole.

'You didn't have the tea,' she said. She turned to face him 'Why not?'

'We forgot,' he said, rather like a penitent child. 'We can have it now though, can't we?'

'But why didn't you have it with her?'

'The time just went. It flew, see. We were sort of— well, you know, *talking*, like.'

Everything he said should have satisfied her, but there was something about the untouched tea that indicated that things had gone radically wrong. Yet why was he so radiantly happy?

The following morning the answer came in the post. Mrs Simmons Actor's Agency was blatantly stamped on the envelope, and Amy hurried to her room to read it before Stan would be ready for his breakfast. The notepaper was white, and most officially stamped, and gave the impression of a summons, which, with its threatening tone, it almost was.

'Dear Miss Evans,' she read, 'I have advised Miss Morgan, in the interests of herself and the Agency, and most probably in yours, to break the contract that I signed with you on her behalf. A contract, as you know, is legally binding, but only if it is entered into in good faith. From Miss Morgan's description of her encounter with your brother, it would seem that we were misled as to the nature of the engagement. I suspect that possibly you are not fully aware of the events that took place on Sunday last in your home, because I gather you were out at the time. And though I find them distasteful to relate, I feel that you must be fully informed so that you will understand why Miss Morgan must terminate her contract.

'Briefly, she came straight to my home from Porth-cawl. She was in a very distressed state. It seems your brother entertained Miss Morgan with a viewing of obscene photographs. Moreover, there were marks on all parts of her body that signalled some kind of assault, and had he not been confined to a wheel-chair your brother surely would have raped her. I do not want to take this matter any further, because it would be hurtful to you, Miss Evans, who, I'm sure, is not to blame. But I suggest that in future you should call on any one of the number of Escort Agencies in Cardiff who would be able to oblige your brother in all his needs, natural or otherwise. I regret that we were not able to enjoy a happier connection. Yours truly, Mrs Simmons.'

In a way Amy was not surprised. But Mrs Simmons' letter wasn't entirely true. In a so-called assault by a cripple, the assaultee must be faintly willing. In any case, from the look on Stan's face when she had returned from the beach, there was no trace of shame or disappointment, or any indication that the love, or whatever it was he had offered Miss Morgan, had met with any opposition. Yet Miss Morgan had gone straight to her agent, on a Sunday too, and in great distress. It was possible, Amy thought, that Miss Morgan had enjoyed their meeting, and had given a performance far beyond the call of duty, and fearful of some report hastened to get in first. Mrs Simmons's letter didn't worry Amy. What disturbed her were the consequences. What was the next move? Miss Morgan would not come again, and for such a part there could be no understudy. With great or indifferent skill, either way, Miss Morgan had queered the pitch for ever.

She had to write to Stan immediately. She had to tell him that in spite of the enjoyment of their meeting she couldn't come again, at least for a very long time. Her poor Mam had taken a bad turn while she was away, and when she returned to Porth a profound guilt had overcome her, especially since she had experienced such profound pleasure. She then continued to describe in general terms how her body had burned in his presence, steering away from all specifics to which she had no clue. It was no mean assignment. She begged him to write to her quickly, 'hot letters,' she wrote. 'Hot, hot, hot,' and to be satisfied for a while with correspondence. She gave him permission to write anything he wished, for everything in the name of love was permissible. She asked for drawings, or copies of the photographs he had shown her. In pen and purple ink, she promised him the earth, but somehow in her heart she knew it would not satisfy him.

*   *   *

She went very early to Porth on the following Thursday. She had little confidence that a letter would be there, and she wanted to spare Mrs Williams and the others the burden of her own disappointment. The cubby-hole was empty. On the bus on the way home she fashioned a rationale why Stan hadn't written, indeed why perhaps he would not write for a few weeks, teasing her, blackmailing her, teaching her a lesson. She had a nagging feeling that she had been through all this country before, when she had waited with patience, despair and anger for her first replies to the advertisement. She did not think she could go through all that again.

She watched Stan closely but there was a little in his behaviour that gave a clue. He was neither sullen nor well-tempered. There was a placid resignation about him and the occasional small and secret smile. After three empty visits to Porth, her hope undiminished, she dared to raise the subject herself.

'When's that nice Blodwen Pugh coming again, then. I should like to meet her proper. Have Gwyneth, too. Make a nice party, I will.' She wanted to go on talking for ever so that he would not have to reply. But the effort of saying just that was enough for her. She could think of no more to say. Her heart hovered for his reply.

'I owe her a letter,' he said. 'I must write. I'll ask her over for next week.'

On the following Thursday she rushed to Porth and an empty cubby-hole. She found it frighteningly easy to hate Stan for the humiliation he was causing her. She hated him for Mrs Williams' disappointment, she hated him for the clerk's sympathy, she hated him above all for Mrs Thomas' commiseration. He now was not to be trusted. She would have to wait a while before she could ask him again. She could not show too much interest in Blodwen lest it should irritate him, and cause him to dispense with the correspondence altogether. Yet she wondered why he didn't write. It was almost a month now since Miss Morgan's performance, and he gave no sign of any aftermath. She decided to write to him again. After all, Blodwen would be worried. She might think he was ill. Anything could have happened. So she wrote, begging for news, giving him once more her tired yet willing body, inch by verbal inch, but it humiliated her, this one-sided offering. He might turn against her completely. So she begged again for a simple communication, and prayed that he was well.

Over the next few weeks she was afraid to go to Porth, and equally fearful to refrain. So she compromised by going very early to avoid the others' expectancy. On her last visit she found herself explaining to the clerk that she didn't really expect a letter. She was just passing by, and thought—well, there's no harm done. She distinctly saw the clerk look at the other tellers and raise his eyes to the ceiling. That's what Mrs Thomas used to say, no doubt. That's how they all start. Poor devils.

She slouched out of the Post Office door. 'I'm mental,' she said to herself. 'That's what I am. And Stan has driven me to it.' But she couldn't hate him long. She would forgive him all the pain for just one luke-warm communication.

The letter-less weeks went by. Somehow, every Thursday she dragged herself to Porth. And then, in desperation, she wrote to him again.

'Dear Stan, Heartbroken I am that you haven't written so many weeks, I cannot count. I am heartbroken too because my poor Mam has passed over. She went peaceful like, in her sleep last night, and I thought, well, I shall write to my Stan to tell him I am free. Free to do what you want with me, see. Write to me, Stan boy, and tell me to come, come, come. Duw, the future is ours. I shall wait your letter for ever. Your beloved Blod.'

She did not think how she would deal with the events that she had herself turned. It was time her rotten Mam died anyway, ruining her life and keeping her from loving and being loved. She'd made her die in her sleep just so as she would be comfortable. But she didn't mourn her. Not a bit.

Amy put down her pen, covered in her own confusion. She felt inside herself that she was going mad, and she wondered whether one could grow out of lunacy as one out-grew unhappiness. 'He's got to answer this one,' she told herself. 'He cannot leave me orphaned without a word.'

In such confidence she rested easy for a while. 'Blodwen never came to tea then,' she said a few days later.

'Her Mam died,' Stan said. 'I'm just writing to her.'

She tried hard to believe him. She would never forgive him if he sent her vainly to Porth again. But the following day he gave her a letter. 'Put it in the post for me Amy,' he said. 'It's for Blodwen.'

She hoped he didn't see her tremble. She had no thoughts of not posting the letter. It had to go to Porth where it belonged. The letter was as much for Mrs Williams and the clerks at the Post Office as it was for her own vindication. She posted it firmly, and she went to Porth at her old and usual time.

She arrived with confidence, glad to see that all the regulars were already there. Mrs Williams, who over the empty weeks had borne the rejection as if it were her own, feared for Amy's sudden confidence. She was jaunty almost. The thought passed through Mrs Williams' mind that such confidence could only come from certain knowledge and that perhaps she had posted a letter to herself. Such a manoeuvre was not unknown amongst those who availed themselves regularly of the poste restante service. Self-deception was often preferable to continual public humiliation. Mrs Williams smiled at Amy sympathetically. She was prepared to understand that, too.

It was Mrs Williams' turn at the grille. Though her Margaret wrote every week she always accepted her letter with surprise and gratitude. She waited until it was Amy's turn, and was not surprised to see a letter handed over the counter. Now it was her turn to simulate, and poor Mrs Williams was not terribly good at it.

'Oh there's wonderful,' she over-enthused. 'A letter at last.'

Amy smiled, but as she walked out of the Post Office she distinctly heard one of the regulars whisper to her neighbour. 'Poor soul. Why even Mrs Thomas would never stoop to that kind of thing.'

She refused to let it upset her. She hurried to the bus stop anxious to get home. Even though the letter she carried was probably the most important of their entire correspondence, she would not break the rules of the production by opening it on the bus. Yet the temptation was gruelling, especially since the bus was late, and held up in a traffic jam over the mountain. She almost ran from the bus stop to the corner of her street and there she paused to get her breath. She found herself shaking. She didn't know why she was afraid or why she was so convinced that she had reason for fear. He had written. How could that be anything but good? Yet she was wary of opening it. She wiped the sweat from her forehead and trudged up the hill to the house. She called 'Stan' as she turned the key in the door. He did not answer. She panicked, running from room to room calling his name. In the kitchen she found a note in Stan's hand. 'Huw called, and we've gone over to the shop. P.S. I shall be staying there for my dinner.'

She sat down with immense relief. There was no need to be frightened any longer. Everything was as it always had been. Huw was his friend, and Gwyneth hers, and every day she would come with the bread, and every Thursday there would be a letter. She and Stan would love as they loved before, ever since the purple ink had flowed between them. Gwyneth would come in for the occasional bruising, and bliss would settle on a cripple and an old maid waiting for the post. Lovingly she opened the letter.

'Dear Miss Pugh.'

She shuddered, not daring to read further. Miss Pugh. Such an address was terminal. The hot tears that for weeks had gathered like pins behind her eyes now flowed freely, hot with anger and regret, crying loud into the empty house, mourning the passing of what was, after all, her own person. There were tears enough for that, and as she cried them out she forced herself to return to the letter and seek the cause of Blodwen's demise.

'I am writing to tell you that I won't be writing to you any more. Because I don't want to deceive you like. It's been very nice writing to you all these weeks, and duw, it was lovely to see you. But it did not satisfy me, just writing the letters, I mean. Your letter about your sad loss came too late, because my heart has been given elsewhere. I have written to you often of our friend Gwyneth. Well, her and me are to be married like in the near future. So I will sign off now, and hope you keep well. Yours faithfully, Stan Evans. P.S. I was really sorry about your Mam.'

Amy saw how the letter trembled, and she realised that her whole body was shaking as if in the throes of a sweeping fit. Her first thought, though it had been Stan's last, was for her poor Mam, and what a waste of a death it had been. Then she thought of the Porthless days ahead, and she wondered whether she should go there just once more to explain to Mrs Williams that her friend had found a house to her satisfaction. Then she thought again of her Mam's needless passing, and then again of empty cubby-holes, and back again to the useless death, and over and over, before the thought of Gwyneth had to find entry, screw-driving its way through all the protecting periphery, until, once arrived, it exploded inside her. And then Amy screamed.

A long piercing cry, that unplugged her brain, draining her skull of all thought, all questioning, leaving behind the solid vacuum of her loss. She was alone in the house, and it was a taste of how it was always going to be. She flung on her coat and ran out of the front door.

She walked away from the cliff. Her mindless steps took her to the cluster of little shops at the far reach of the sands. The butcher's shop was now specialising in cold cuts with an eye on the trippers. The flower shop that had provided wreaths for her Mam and her Dad had gone out of business and nothing had replaced it. A little mini-mart had sprouted on the corner, swallowing the site and the gossip of the old haberdashery store. The little book shop was still there, but now it only sold paper doyleys. But holding its solid and proud ground at the end of the parade was Fullertons, the sweet shop, that so many wounds ago had taken from Amy's tight little hand the pennies she had taken from her Mam's tight little purse. She went inside. She looked at the counter. It had retained its old symmetry to the last stick of liquorice. A clutch of sherbet to start off the line, giving way to an assortment of bull's eyes. A narrow wooden slat divided these from the gum-drops, which were themselves sealed off with liquorice sticks. And right at the end of the line lay tissue-wrapped Porthcawl, in all its pink and sticky glory. She put her hand up to her nose. Its stubbiness itched suddenly like an old scar.

'A stick of rock, please,' she said. She heard the squeak in her voice, and she quickly swallowed the child-lump in her throat. 'It's for my niece,' she added quickly, ashamed suddenly of her false teeth and her total lack of equipment to deal with the only reliable tool of her childhood.

The young girl at the counter was too pretty to have ever needed a rock-dependency. She shrugged and wrapped the stick. Amy noticed the refinement. In the old days it was just handed neat over the counter, simultaneously with the penny taken from the other side. Now its price was twenty times that much. Amy wondered what ugly children used nowadays for solace.

She unwrapped it as she walked towards the cliff, tearing the brown wrapping into pieces, scattering it on the grass to spite her Mam. She made her way across the rock, sucking desperately on the pink stick. A piece caught in her throat and she retched on it, choking on her childhood. The perching gulls took off as she approached. She felt like the plague. In her heart she had brought them back the ugly little Amy of so many sticks of rock ago. She sucked. It took a little time for Porthcawl to show bright and clear, and when it did, the magic struggled free. She kept her hand on one side of the stick, and sucking, she walked to the sea. She had reached an age when she popped an indigestion tablet into her mouth after every meal, an age when her frock caught in the fold of her bottom as she walked, yet as she sucked and sucked, and proclaimed 'Cawl' beneath her tongue, she was a child again, freed from the prison on the hill, and with the rock and the gulls for comfort. With her eyes she followed the makings of one enormous wave, and she inhaled deeply, holding her breath as it gathered, then sighing it out as it broke and scattered on the rock. She felt strangely peaceful. Gwyneth came into her mind without pain. She thought of the last months and how her perilous deception had opened her brother's heart. She knew that the un-locking had been her own doing. She understood, too, that she had opened it for Gwyneth. But she was reconciled.

That evening they told her. Gwyneth brought Stan home, and Huw with them. Amy had guessed that that evening they would break the news, so for long before they arrived she had practised her reaction in the mirror. She had to affect both surprise and pleasure. The first would be difficult, she knew, but neither did she have confidence in the second. On the beach, the prospect of Stan's marriage had pleased her. But it had been in thought only. Now, soon to be confronted with the flesh of it, with the reality of their declaration, she could not trust herself to be delighted. The more she practised the more affected her expression, so she decided to let it be until they told her.

She was preparing supper in the kitchen when they arrived. On the quiet she had prepared for all of them, to give the impression that her cupboard was always full. Gwyneth was a lucky woman—the Evans had class in Porthcawl—and Amy hoped Gwyneth was not unmindful of it. She heard Stan's key in the lock, and a hubbub in the hall.

'Amy?'

It was Gwyneth who called her. Amy frowned. It was Stan's right to announce his arrival in their house. With Gwyneth stealing his line, there was a threat of take-over.

'I'm in the kitchen,' she shouted. 'Stan all right?'

'More than all right,' he said, as he wheeled himself into the kitchen with Gwyneth and Huw beside him.

Amy turned round. 'Huw,' she said, 'there's nice to see you now. Will you stay for a bit of supper?' She turned quickly back to the sink, fearful of a bad performance.

'You got enough then?' Gwyneth said. 'I'll say this about you Amy. You're like your Mam. Always keep a good table.'

A back-handed compliment that, Amy thought, but a good start nevertheless. She had to turn round and look at them, or stop what she was doing to talk to them, or it might look as if she was deliberately avoiding any communication. Yet she could not turn around. She did not trust the heat behind her eyes or her trembling hands.

'We've brought the champagne for our supper,' Stan said.

Now she had to make a move. What Stan had said was not a daily declaration. She had to react.

'Champagne?' she said to the sink. Then, turning on a whispered prayer, 'What we celebrating then?'

Gwyneth looked at Stan, and Stan at Gwyneth, and both giggled. Amy felt a painful isolation.

'They've got something to tell you,' Huw said. 'Go on then,' turning to Stan.

'You say it, Huw,' Stan said.

'No. It's your place.'

'Go on Gwyneth,' Stan said.

'It's you to speak,' Gwyneth giggled, 'like Huw said.'

179

'Well make up your minds, then,' Amy said, thankful for a reprieve however slight. She turned back to the sink.

She heard whispering behind her. The onus of news-breaking was undoubtedly falling on Huw, which was probably why he'd been brought round in the first place. She heard him coughing.

'Amy,' he said.

'I'm listening.'

'Well, um, you see,' then in one quick apologetic breath, 'Stan and Gwyneth's getting married like.'

Now, though empty of delight, she had to turn. 'Duw,' she said. The tears began to flow. She didn't mind them. Tears could be tears of joy, and she hoped they'd be generous enough to interpret them as such. 'Duw,' she said again, thinking what a bloody silly word it was, since it said everything and nothing at all.

'You pleased then?' Stan said nervously.

She couldn't say 'Duw' again, so she just nodded her head.

Then she stepped forward and formally kissed her prospective sister-in-law on the cheek. Then down to Stan's forehead.

'Poor Blodwen,' she said.

Stan blushed, flustered.

'Who's Blodwen, then?' Gwyneth shouted, 'when the cows come home?'

Amy had not mentioned Blodwen out of malice. It was by way of commiserating with herself. She had assumed quite naturally that Stan had told Gwyneth the Blodwen story.

'Who's this Blodwen, then?' Gwyneth shouted again, and Amy thought how like a fish-wife she looked.

'Sorry I spoke,' Amy said, making matters much worse.

Blodwen had now undeniably become the other woman. Poor Gwyneth, who in her late and unflowered years could hardly accommodate the notion of being the one and only, was now prematurely confronted with possible adultery. 'Disgusting,' she hissed.

'No, it's nothing,' Stan pleaded with her. Then to Amy, 'What you want to go and make trouble for?'

She was glad she had an excuse to cry, which she did loudly and without restraint.

'Oh I'm sorry, Amy,' Stan tried to make himself heard.

'You'd better tell us about this Blodwen,' Huw said, on his sister's side. Amy's sobs subsided. She was clearing the air for Stan's explanation. Let him do it, she thought, as he should have done in the first place.

'It was nothing really,' he said. 'Blodwen Pugh. From Porth she was. I only saw her once. But we wrote, see, for quite a long time.'

'How long?' Gwyneth asked, testing the weight of the competition.

'About four or five months, I suppose. But it was one-sided like. She was nagging me all the time. Wanting to get married like.'

You loathsome liar, Amy thought, but how could she contradict him?

'So in the end I didn't write any more, except to tell her last week that,' he shuffled in his chair, 'well, I was in love with Gwyneth, see.'

'When did you see her then?' Gwyneth said, who was the last to let a sleeping dog lie.

'It's a few weeks ago, wasn't it, Amy?'

Amy nodded.

'What was she like then?' Gwyneth was relentless.

'You silly bugger,' Amy shouted at her. 'It's all over,

so forget it.' Amy's outburst sobered Gwyneth who went over to comfort her.

'What about the champagne, then?' Huw said. 'And you can say what you like, Gwyneth Price, soon to be Gwyneth Evans, I'm taking off my arm.' And there and then he unscrewed it in front of them, laying it on the kitchen table.

Gwyneth shielded Amy from the amputation. It was, to say the least, an unusual accompaniment to an announcement of marriage.

'That's right, Huw,' Stan said. 'No harm in being comfortable.'

'I'll get the glasses,' Amy said getting up.

Huw took the champagne with his one hand and deftly urged the cork. The wine was warm from Gwyneth's clutching, and the cork plopped sadly on to the mat.

'Bit too warm it is,' Huw said, pouring it out. 'But good enough to celebrate. Here's to Stan and Gwyneth,' he said, raising his glass in Amy's direction, 'and to a long and happy marriage to both of them.'

Amy sipped from her glass. She was not feeling too well, but she steeled herself to stand steady, and she tried to ignore the gathering weakness in her knees.

'And here's to Amy and Huw,' Stan said. 'Our family.'

Amy was grateful to sit down. 'It's the champagne,' she said, noting how the others watched her. 'I'll go and lie down a bit.' But she sat there still, knowing that standing would be a risk. But she had to try. The effort unhinged her. She fell forward on to the table, her forehead blocked by Huw's wooden palm.

'Get water, Gwyneth,' Huw said. 'It's all the excitement.'

Gwyneth fussed around her splashing water on her

face. Stan wheeled his chair beside her, and they all looked at her.

Amy felt them around her. The sickness had gone. Inside her head was a strange clarity. But she knew how exposed she was, how unprotected her stubby nose and jutting chin, how magnified they were to their close and anxious scrutiny. By waking, she would proclaim those ugly features as her own. It was better to retreat into Blodwen once more, just one more time, she promised herself, to gather strength to take Amy Evans to the wedding.

For this purpose, perhaps, she took to her bed the following day. She had tried to get up, but her legs would not hold her. Gwyneth brought the bread in the morning and waited for the doctor to come.

'So it's Amy for a change,' he said. 'Never been ill in her life.'

Gwyneth waited with Stan in the kitchen while Dr Rhys took his bag to Amy's room. Gwyneth had made her own diagnosis. 'Over-excitement it is,' she said to Stan, and to herself, 'Jealousy, that's what it is. Disgusting.'

Stan was strangely calm. He viewed the turn of events with the detachment of a survivor. 'Hope we won't have to alter our plans, cariad,' he said.

'We've got a whole month,' Gwyneth re-assured him. 'She'll be up and about in a few days.'

An hour had passed and Dr Rhys was still in the bedroom, and Stan thought that perhaps Gwyneth didn't know everything.

'Shall I go and have a look?' she said.

'No. You make the tea. She'll like a cup when he's gone.'

They waited. The longer they waited, the more confused Gwyneth was in her diagnosis. You couldn't pin-point jealousy. The pulse nor the heartbeat would betray it. 'It's psychological,' she said to herself, 'and psychological business takes longer.'

It was another half hour before they heard Amy's door open. When Dr Rhys came into the kitchen he looked serious and defeated.

'Can't make it out,' he said. 'I've examined her head to foot. Can't find a thing. Yet it's true that she cannot stand on her feet, leave alone walk. I can't fathom it myself. Never seen a case like it before.'

'What we going to do then?' Stan said.

'Better wait and see I suppose.'

'There's nothing the matter with her, I can tell you. She's had a bit of excitement,' Gwyneth volunteered, hoping to give him a clue. 'We're getting married, you know, me and Stan.'

'She told me that,' Dr Rhys said, without congratulations, 'but whatever it is, it's nothing to do with that. Now don't you get this psychology nonsense into your head, Miss Price. It's very dangerous. No,' he paused, 'there's something the matter for sure, but I can't for the life of me find it. I'll come in tomorrow. See how she is. If she's not changed we'll have to get a specialist from Cardiff. So you're getting married,' he said referring to the matter at its proper time. 'Well, congratulations then. When is it to be?'

'Next month, we thought,' Stan said. 'But Amy has to be better.'

'She'll get up for your wedding, no doubt,' Dr Rhys said, though her body had given him no reason why it should.

'Looking after your chest, then, Stan? You'll see us all out, you will.'

Gwyneth saw him to the door. 'Have you told us everything?' she said, positive that the doctor was withholding information. Doctors knew everything. Perhaps the news about Amy was bad and it was better untold. 'You can tell me,' she added.

'I'd tell you or anybody else,' Dr Rhys said simply, 'if only I knew. But it stumps me. We shall have to see.'

Gwyneth took Amy's tea to her room. 'Daft, isn't it?' Amy said. 'I feel all right, but I can't stand up. He can't find anything wrong, and I can tell you girl, between you and me, he didn't half look. And the questions he asked. Blushing I was.'

'What sort of questions?'

'I'm not telling. Rude they were.'

'Suit yourself,' Gwyneth said, turning on her heel.

'Gwyneth,' Amy called her back, 'will you be able to look after Stan while I'm in bed?'

'Able?' Gwyneth said. 'I shall be doing it for the rest of my life, shan't I?' She smiled. 'You're the one to be looked after, anyway. I'll make arrangements in the shop. I'll stay till you get better Amy. I'll cutch down on the couch in the parlour. You've got to get up for our wedding, mind.'

Amy knew why she couldn't get up, and if her reasoning was correct, then she would not walk again. Certainly not until after the wedding, and even that was doubtful. She did not care very much. She was simply curious as to why it had happened at all. On the beach, she had confronted the impending marriage, and she had been content. She had seen herself in the role of go-between, grooming Stan for such an eventuality. It was natural that she should feel a little jealous when her star pupil ceased to need her. But there was joy in having prepared him and, on the beach, it had made her content. Why then, when the events had turned into words and flat champagne, did the hurt assault her? 'I don't mind really,' she'd wanted to tell them. 'It's just my body protesting.' But she was not angry with such a protest, overwhelming as it was. Her body had to do what what it had to do, irrespective of how her fancy thoughts were dwelling. Her body would not take her to the wedding, and that was that. So be it, she thought. I'll stay in bed till my body's ready. Besides, it was pleasant being waited upon. For the first time in her life she was actually being cared for. She found some pleasure in watching Gwyneth unknowingly pay for her match-making services.

Over the next few days Gwyneth would often sit with her and tell her of her wedding plans. The pains would shoot through Amy's legs and she was satisfied that her body was going about its business.

'And what will you be wearing then, girl?' Gwyneth said. 'Buy something new, won't you?'

Amey smiled. 'I hope I shall be able to go,' she said.

'You've got two whole weeks yet. Bound to be better.'

'Better?' Amy said. 'According to Dr Rhys, I'm not ill.'

The specialist had been called, and like Dr Rhys he had found nothing organically wrong. But unlike Dr Rhys he proposed an emotional paralysis, and Gwyneth was delighted. Dr Rhys scoffed behind the specialist's back, but he had no alternative to offer, and Amy felt sorry for him. 'What's the cure then?' he had asked. The old man prescribed some pills. He was cagey in his explanation of what they were. 'They'll settle you a bit,' was all he could say.

For a week Amy had taken them, and they'd made her light-headed and carefree. In her mind she would have soared, but her legs remained firmly planted on the ground. The body was winning, and Amy didn't mind.

'You'll have to get married without me,' she said.

'Rubbish,' Gwyneth said. 'You talk as if you're going to be in bed for the rest of your life.'

'That'll make two cripples for you to look after,' Amy laughed.

'I don't think that's very funny, Amy Evans,' Gwyneth said. She straightened the counterpane and she took Amy's hand. Any physical contact was a rare gesture for Gwyneth. 'You're going to get better, girl,' she said. Then acting on her own diagnosis, 'I'm not taking Stan away from you, girl, we're all going to be together.'

Amy smiled. Paralysed as she was, she felt like a conqueror, and for the first time she tasted the colonising power of a cripple. Now she understood Stan's secret smiles, his content, his smugness even. She was closer to Stan than Gwyneth could ever be. You'll take my Stan, she thought, and you'll take me too.

So she indulged in her withdrawal, receiving daily bulletins from Stan and Gwyneth as to the wedding arrangements. The church had been booked, and the hall afterwards for the reception. Even a band had been engaged. A small affair, Gwyneth had said, more respectable like. Don't want to be wasting money now, do we? A tea-dance like, with pastries from her own shop. For the honeymoon, Stan had set his heart on a cruise, and Amy's legs shot with pain again, for Gwyneth was treading on her dreams.

The counterpane was spread with travel brochures and maps. Gwyneth recited all the exotic cruise possibilities, taking her time to tell Amy of their decision, rambling on through latitude and longtitude, while Amy concentrated on the pain in her legs and didn't listen to a single word. She just waited for Gwyneth to stop, and when she did she blandly put the question that had been itching her ever since she took to her bed.

'And who's going to look after me, then?' she asked, 'when you're away.'

Gwyneth was flummoxed. 'Duw, girl,' she said, breathless, 'you'll be looking after yourself, won't you?'

'Like this?' Amy said. 'In bed?'

'Now you'll be up and about after the wedding,' Gwyneth said. She didn't want to explode, but she was close.

'What makes you think that?'

'Now look here, girl,' Gwyneth said angrily, 'there's nothing the matter with you that a bit of pulling yourself together won't cure. You've had a doctor and a specialist and they can't find anything wrong. You've had tablets, and I've looked after you, and you know bloody well you could get up if you had a mind to it. You're just jealous of the wedding, that's all.'

It was out, and neither of them knew what to do with it. The silence was dreadful. It was Amy's lack of comeback that disturbed Gwyneth most. It was almost a proof of her innocence.

'I'm sorry, then,' Gwyneth said. 'Terribly sorry. I shouldn't have spoke. I didn't mean it. I'll look after you. You're not to worry about that.' She took Amy's hand, and Amy gave her a Stan smile. 'There's good you are to me, Gwyneth,' she said, and when Gwyneth had gone, she snuggled in her bed and said to herself, 'Duw, there's lovely it is being a cripple.'

Stan was making his preparations too. Amy could hear him in his room. She wondered what he would do with his mattress literature, whether he would dispose of it, or somehow incorporate it into his marriage. Perhaps they would have viewing parties every Saturday night. Lovely.

Gwyneth came in with the tea. 'Don't shout at me, Amy,' she said, 'but I went to Pugh's and I bought you a dress. Now after you've had your tea, you're going to stand up and you're going to try it on.'

'Oh Gwyneth, you know I can't do that.'

'You're going to try, girl, and if not, then you'll do it sitting down.' She put the tray on the bed. 'It's a lovely dress. Pale blue, Stan said it would go with your eyes.'

'Has Stan seen it then?'

'Seen it?' she laughed. 'He went and chose it. Chose the hat, too. Said he knew your taste better than anyone.'

The pain ceased in Amy's legs. 'There's good you are to me, Gwyneth,' she said.

After tea, Gwyneth brought in the dress and with great ceremony laid it on the bed. It was wrapped, and only its colour was visible through the tissue paper. 'Now you'll try it on first, and then you'll look at it,' Gwyneth said. 'Looks nothing on a hanger.'

Amy helped herself as best she could out of bed, and with Gwyneth's support she leaned against the brass rail. 'I can't stand,' she said. 'My legs won't take me.'

'Hang on to the rail, then, and shut your eyes.' Gwyneth threw the dress over Amy's head, and Amy stuck her arms through one by one. Gwyneth straightened it out. 'Lovely,' she said. 'Like it was tailor-made. Now the hat.'

She went out of the room again to return with the hat box. 'Keep your eyes shut now, girl.' She put it on Amy's head.

Stan had chosen well. There was a cheval mirror in the corner and Amy dragged it over into Amy's line of vision. 'Open now,' she said.

Amy viewed herself with wonder. She did not speak for a long while, and then she whispered, 'Look like a bride, I do.'

* * *

In the magazines that Amy read, a red-letter day was heralded by the phrase, 'At last the great day dawned.' And when an acute pain in the legs woke Amy on the day of the wedding, it was this thought that passed through her mind before she dealt with the pain. She rubbed her legs and wanted to cry. She reached across to the bed-side table and took a handful of pills, many more than the specialist had prescribed, and she lay back willing the pain to go away. And as it ebbed, fear took its place.

It was beginning to irritate her with its constant calling. It knew bloody well she could do nothing about it. With this thought, the pills took over. Her head became light as her pulse beat faster, and a gentle euphoria suffused her. The great day has dawned, she thought again.

Downstairs, she could hear noises. Soon Huw would be coming up with her tea. He had taken over from Gwyneth the night before. Gwyneth, no doubt, was at this very moment scrubbing all her unmentionables, and stuffing all her orifices with talcum powder. Then she would put on her knickers, 'something blue,' she had told Amy, 'Frenchies they are. Disgusting.' Then her white dress. Gwyneth had insisted on that and who better entitled than she. But Amy didn't want to think about that. Such thoughts led to terrible places, Stan's bed being the first. She was glad she had taken the pills. They seemed to blunt the edge of perilous thought.

She heard Huw on the stairs with the tray. She covered her bosom with the bed-jacket, and then on second thoughts she cast it aside. The great day had dawned, and it was hers as well. Might as well make the most of it.

He knocked gently at the door. 'Come in,' she said, her voice choked with dependency. Huw was shy. He avoided looking at her, and he put the tray on the bed sideways. She was glad he had his arm on. She stretched out to take it. 'There now, Huw,' she said, 'look at him blushing, and you a married man too.'

He looked at her. His eyes watered with pity. 'Can't you get up, Amy?' he said.

She shook her head without regret.

'It's no good, Huw. I won't be going. But I'll put on my dress, I will,' she added hastily, 'and my hat, and I'll sit up in my bed, and I'll pretend I'm in chapel. Have to give me a hand though, Huw.'

He touched her fingers warily. 'Drink your tea, then,' he said.

He waited, trying not to look at her barely-covered breasts and working out where to put his claw when he would carry her. He hoped she would cover her chest.

'I'm ready,' she said, putting down the cup, and stretching out her arms towards him. And he could not help but respond. He was glad now that her breasts were bare, that he could feel their warmth as he carried her, his handicap touching hers. He helped her wash, as if she were a child, spraying her with talc and perfumes, then he carried her back to her room and laid out her wedding clothes on the bed.

'I'll be back,' he said. 'I'll bring Stan up so's you can see him.'

He left the door slightly open and Amy could hear Stan singing. The Minstrel Boy was going to the war again, and she couldn't help thinking with a certain pleasure that it was a rather inept choice for a wedding morn. Moreover, Stan had him going to the war twice and three times, to be found each time in the ranks of three-syllabled death.

She looked at the dress Stan had bought her. She was delighted at his choice. It was an ensemble she might have worn for her own nuptials. Silly bugger, that Gwyneth, she thought. White indeed. Fancy parading her locked and barred portals at her time of life. Nothing to be proud of, I'm sure, Gwyneth Price. Only goes to show that no one ever wanted you. Not even a parlee voo.

It took her a long time to get ready. She heard Huw manoeuvring Stan's chair up the stairway. When she was ready, leaning against the bed, she took the locket from between her breasts and let it hang loud and clear on the front of her dress. Then she called for them to come in.

Huw wheeled Stan into the bedroom. For a long while, brother and sister stared at each other, then at the floor, for both, at this moment, in each other's eyes, were naked.

'How do I look then?' Stan said when the silence had become unbearable.

'Going into battle I am,' he laughed, much louder than was necessary and begging her to understand.

'You've got a new suit.'

'You've got a new dress.'

They were silent again. Huw fidgeted. 'I've got an orchid for you,' he said. He gave it to her like a love token.

'Where shall I put it?' Amy said.

'On the lace in the front.'

'But that'll hide the locket.'

'On the shoulder then,' Stan said.

As she was fixing it, he fingered the locket. 'Our Mam's, wasn't it?' he said. 'Anything inside?'

'It's empty,' she said quickly. 'Like it was with our Mam.'

'I shall by one of those for Gwyneth,' he said 'She can put my photo in it.'

'You're daft,' Amy said.

Again they stared at each other. 'The car's waiting,' Stan said.

Amy swallowed. 'Good luck then, cariad,' she said.

Stan turned away his head. 'We'll be back after chapel,' he said.

Huw lifted Amy into the bed and straightened her dress and her hat. 'Duw,' he said, 'there's lovely you look. Like a bride, you do.'

She heard the front door close. If she turned her head she could see the wedding car through the window. Huw was lifting Stan into the back seat, while the chauffeur was trying to close the boot on the chair. He tried this way and that, with mounting impatience, until it was clear to him that the boot would not close. Angrily he stuffed the white ribbon in his pocket. The tail-end of his newly polished limousine was at plebeian odds with his beribboned front, and he drove off quickly, as if ashamed of his cargo.

Amy lay back on the pillows, travelling with her groom. She could not imagine that he was happy, or that he was confident in his decision. All she allowed herself to feel was his fear. She saw him installed in the front pews of the chapel, his gentle hands trembling. She was glad she was unable to go. The congregation must be speculating on her absence. Her illness had been spread abroad by Gwyneth, along with her diagnosis, and no doubt most of the wedding guests accepted it with greater and lesser degrees of malice. Though some there were, she knew, who thought that after all these years she had caught it from Stan. In a way she had, though not especially 'caught'. Rather had she invited it, gatecrashing on his handicap, an uninvited guest to his Gwyneth-wheeled future. They would be happy together, the three of them.

She heard the gulls cry, and turning her head she just caught their landing. Dozens of them were perched on the distant rock that bounded the bay, squalling their touch-down, pecking the salty reliable runway that would be at their service for ever. They perched, and she looked away, as she had looked away as a child, creeping back to the anger-house on the hill, knowing that they would wait there until she was gone. Gentlemen they were, gulls.

She fingered the counterpane. Gwyneth must have arrived by now, standing at the chapel door, the wash-day brightness of her filling the aisle. An over-ripe virgin who had put it all by for this day. Open it tonight, then, Amy thought, and you'll find it's all gone bad. Kept it too long you did, girl. Now it's not fit for human consumption.

She fingered the locket on her neck, and steered her perilous thoughts away from the chapel. Inside, veiled with a lock of hair, lay the Blodwen deception. That, together with the red-ribboned pile of letters in her dressing-table drawer, were the sole pieces of evidence that could prove the conspiracy. Stan must never know about it. How could he live with the knowledge that his sister knew him so intimately. Yet she couldn't bring herself to destroy the evidence. It was hers. She had not only deceived Stan for it; she had been well on the way to deceiving herself. She had worked for those letters. She was entitled. I'll keep them locked in the drawer, she thought, and I'll wear the locket round my neck until I die. Bed-ridden as she was, she assumed that Stan would go before her, and then the line would end, and what was around her neck would be a fable.

The pain in her legs was returning, willing her back to the church. She tried to fight it, to stay chained to her cosy cripple-bed, listening to the cry of the gulls, and knowing that they perched there still. She was tempted to look back at the rock, but an Orpheus-fear restrained her. Now the pain shot into her thighs, and willed her to face her own rejection.

Gwyneth was standing by her Stan, with a healthy wholeness enough for both of them. Three of us, it'd better be, Amy thought, and she wanted to look at the sea again. Yet she knew she must not turn her head, else the gulls would take a swift and terrible revenge. She had to trust them to be perched there still, until the wound of the ceremony healed close.

The vicar bowed towards the congregation. 'If any man knows of some impediment', he said. Now the tears fell hot down Amy's cheeks, and she screamed to drown his words, but his warning was loud and ominous. 'Or forever hold his peace.'

'Yes. In God's name I do,' she screamed into the empty room. 'He's bespoke to Blodwen Pugh of Porth, he is.'

Now she broke uncontrollably, sobbing aloud, as the gulls on the rock cawed the desolate echo of her pain. Her legs throbbed, summoning her back to the ceremony. There would be a time for weeping, a time for hate, and a time, if there were cruel time enough, for forgiveness. So she forced herself to watch her brother and her only and most treacherous friend as the vicar declared them man and wife.

It was over. The Evans litter, if not multiplied, would at least end on a double line. Gwyneth turned to Stan's chair. Stan looked up at her, and cradling her face with his hands, he brought it down gently to his lips. Amy forced herself to watch it. In their kiss she had a glimpse of the land afar off. She was ignorant of what sin she had committed, save that of siblinghood, that had denied her entry, nor what particular virtue had granted Gwyneth a visa. She only knew that she had made it all possible, that it was she who had led her fickle brother through the wilderness of his passion.

The pain in her legs subsided, and now a burning weakness suffused her body, a gentle melting of muscle, a numbing of the nerve. The sickly fear returned, the terror that she had put aside ever since she had taken to her bed. Now it slithered like a feathered drum-brush on her heart, and she knew its cause. She held the locket close in her fevered hand, willing it to disappear, to melt into the soul's foundry. With her ebbing strength she crawled from the bed, dragging herself along the floor to the dressing-table. Once there, she reached painfully for the drawer, fumbling amongst the lavender bags for her red-ribboned love. And as she pulled them out they broke their silken chain and scattered over the floor. 'I didn't mean that,' she whispered. 'That's not what I meant at all.'

She tried to gather them together, but most of them were beyond her feeble reach. She ached with the pain that their discovery would cause, and desperately she reached out to touch them. But she knew the attempt was futile for she had neither time nor place to hide them. She was dying wreathed in her own sad strata-gems, all that would remain to tell her story. 'Forgive me, Stan,' she whispered. 'I did it for love, cariad.'

She knew that she was ready now to look back at the gulls, and she asked for strength to raise her body and turn her head to the sea. She had never seen the gulls so white and beautiful. 'Cawl,' she pleaded. 'It is Amy's time.'

They screeched, keening their loss, and fidgeting into formation they took off in fury, swooping down over the cliff. For a while they hovered, then, wheeling slowly, they glided over the sea, nudging the horizon with their angry cortège.

A
GERMAN
Love Story

ROLF HOCHHUTH

This is the poignant story of two very
ordinary human beings whose natural
instincts proved stronger than their fear
of the inhuman penalties decreed by
Hitler and imposed by Himmler and his
Gestapo. It is also a razor-sharp and
ironical study of Nazism as a worldwide
phenomenon not specific to Germany
alone.

Rolf Hochhuth is already known for
the controversial nature of his plays; and
A GERMAN LOVE STORY, his most
thought-provoking work, can best be
described as a documentary novel. He
has met and interviewed the survivors of
the true and brutally tragic story – the
woman whose love sent her lover to the
gallows, the men who built the gallows
and watched his execution, the local
Nazis who denounced the ill-starred
couple and who still live and prosper in
the idyllic South German village where
Stasiek Zasada, a Polish prisoner of war,
was judicially strangled nearly forty
years before.

FICTION   0 349 11698 9   £1.95

(ABACUS)

GOD ON THE ROCKS
Jane Gardam

A hot, seemingly endless summer between the wars, in a small seaside town in north-east England: this is the background to Margaret Marsh's slow awakening to the world around her. A child caught up in the drama of the dance of life and death, Margaret observes the sexual rituals of the adults who are part of her daily life. Her father, preaching the doctrine of the Primal Saints; her mother, bitterly nostalgic for what might have been; Charles and Binkie, brother and sister, atrophied in a game of words like flies in amber; and, the inevitable catalyst, Lydia, the Marches' maid, given to sateen and the smell of Devonshire Violets and the vulgar enjoyment of life: all these contribute to Margaret's shattering moment of truth when the dam breaks. It is not only God who is on the rocks at the coming of summer's end . . .

FICTION   0 349 11406 4   £1.95

A SELECTION OF TITLES AVAILABLE FROM ABACUS

NON-FICTION

PRISONERS OF PAIN	Dr. Arthur Janov	£3.50
OTHER WORLDS	Paul Davies	£2.50
THE SCHUMACHER LECTURES	Satish Kumar	£2.50
THE OLD STRAIGHT TRACK	Alfred Watkins	£2.50
SEX IN HISTORY	Reay Tannahill	£2.95
SMALL IS BEAUTIFUL	E. F. Schumacher	£1.95
TOUCH THE EARTH	T. McLuhan	£3.95
THE ARABS	Thomas Kiernan	£2.95
TO HAVE OR TO BE	Erich Fromm	£1.75
IRELAND: A HISTORY	Robert Kee	£5.95

FICTION

A STANDARD OF BEHAVIOUR	William Trevor	£1.95
THE EMPEROR OF THE AMAZON	Marcio Souza	£2.50
THE WAPSHOT SCANDAL	John Cheever	£2.50
GOD ON THE ROCKS	Jane Gardam	£1.95
A GERMAN LOVE STORY	Rolf Hochhuth	£1.95
JACK IN THE BOX	William Kotzwinkle	£1.95
DANCE OF THE TIGER	Björn Kurtén	£1.95
KINDERGARTEN	P. S. Rushforth	£1.95

All Abacus books are available at your local bookshop or newsagent, or can be ordered direct from the publisher. Just tick the titles you want and fill in the form below.

Name _____

Address _____

_____

Write to Abacus Books, Cash Sales Department, P.O. Box 11, Falmouth, Cornwall TR10 9EN.

Please enclose a cheque or postal order to the value of the cover price plus:

UK: 45p for the first book plus 20p for the second book and 14p for each additional book ordered to a maximum charge of £1.63.

BFPO & EIRE: 45p for the first book plus 20p for the second book and 14p for the next 7 books, thereafter 8p per book.

OVERSEAS: 75p for the first book and 21p per copy for each additional book.

Abacus Books reserve the right to show new retail prices on covers which may differ from those previously advertised in the text or elsewhere, and to increase postal rates in accordance with the P.O.